Feb 2022.

For the lovely 'And.

Happy Birthday! ... I hope
you enjoy my little adventure.

High paw waves!

Barnaby & him!

X .

BARNABY
and the
DUMPSTER DIVERS

BARNABY
and the
DUMPSTER DIVERS

by
CHRIS MORENO

ILLUSTRATIONS BY GRAHAM MCLUSKY

2021

BARNABY
and the
DUMPSTER DIVERS

by
CHRIS MORENO

ILLUSTRATIONS BY GRAHAM MCLUSKY

A BARNABY PUG DOG ADVENTURE

First published in Great Britain 2021

Published by MIGHTY PENS LTD
in association with BOOKAHOLICS PUBLISHING
Lincolnshire, LN11 7HT

ISBN: 978-1-8382882-2-8

Page design: Pageset Ltd, High Wycombe, Buckinghamshire.
Printed by Short Run Press Ltd, Sowton Industrial Estate,
Exeter, Devon.

CONTENTS

ACKNOWLEDGEMENTS

Thanasis Corfu

Anne MacLachlan

Anna Thomas

Rosie M

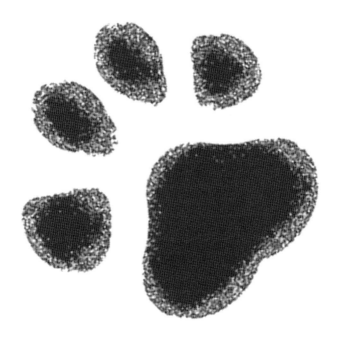

A BARNABY PUG DOG ADVENTURE

For:

Heather

Henry

Anna

James

Vee

Dumpster diving definition:

The practice of searching through large metal dustbins foraging for discarded but still usable objects such as food or clothes.

CHAPTER ONE

'SUMMER HOLIDAY'

W ell George," said my mother, "this all looks very nice. I think we have found the perfect place for our summer holiday."

George looked around the charming lounge with its large comfy settees, a drinks cabinet and the biggest television he had ever seen.

"Just look at this!"

"I know," said Dorothy, "the view is spectacular!"

"No, I mean the television it's… oh never mind!" Said George.

The rented villa sat at the top of a steep hillside. One wall was made of thick glass. You could look out to the sea and watch the gentle waves lapping against each other as they rolled invitingly onto the beach. There were fishing boats of various sizes tied up alongside each other, bobbing up and down in the clear blue waters. Towards one end of the beach sat an old taverna where several of the boat owners nattered while enjoying a cold beer or Greek ouzo.

I jumped up at the lounge window to have a look. Ever since I was a baby, I have loved water. Now that I am nearly three and, if I say so myself, all grown up, I love it even more.

"What do you think Barnaby?" Said my mother. "Do you think you are going to enjoy this holiday?"

"Woof-woof, woof, woof, woof!" I barked.

Barnaby and the Dumpster Divers

For those of you who are now confused, I should explain that I am a dog. Not just any dog. I am a pug dog. There are three things that pug dogs love apart from their owners.

Food, sunshine and swimming in a beautiful pool. Additionally, there are three things that every pug dog owner should know. We are incredibly stubborn, enormously greedy and very, very loving.

Having seen the beautiful swimming pool from the window it was apparent that I was going to be spoilt. Yes, I was in pug dog heaven. I thought it was going to be the best holiday ever. Little did I know how soon I would change my mind.

"Dorothy, why don't I take Mr. B for a little walk while you start to unpack?"

"This sudden need to take Barnaby for a walk would have nothing to do with the taverna I can see on the beach below, would it, George?"

"Taverna?" Said my father quizzically, "I don't think I noticed!"

"No, of course not," said my mother with scant sarcasm. "Ok, off you go, but don't be too long, it's getting late."

The beach! I was so excited I started to run around chasing my tail. Now, a lot of people wonder why pug dogs chase their tail and truth be told we don't know, it just feels so good!

"George!" Shouted my mother as we headed out the door, "make sure it's only one beer! Now skedaddle before I change my mind!"

We started off down the hillside, treading carefully to avoid nettles and local creepy crawlies. There were loads of spiders all wondering aimlessly about. It reminded me of a joke, that George had told. 'Why did the spider crawl into the computer? He had to check his website!' A silly joke, but it helped me pick my way through these leggy creatures. Either side of the path were olive trees, with their twisted, knotted trunks giving a feeling of long held pain. Slowly, the path began to straighten as we emerged from the forestry and headed towards the beach.

Running on ahead I could see the taverna. People were chatting noisily, the odd burst of laughter could be heard, dampened only by the noise of the waves as they rolled onto the sand. George, now slightly out of breath, caught up with me as we arrived at the front of the stone building, built so long ago.

"Wait for me Mr. B, remember you've got four legs, I've only got two!"

I would have liked to have told him that his legs were ten times longer than mine, and if he did a bit more exercise, he would be ahead of me!

Outside of this old watering hole were eight rickety tables, each one surrounded with rusty, old, crumbled chairs. George carefully sat down, and I nestled under his chair, keeping out of the sun.

We took in the glorious views. Laying idle on the beach were a couple of old collapsed fishing boats. Children with bamboo sticks were playing at being pirates, climbing up onto these mangled boats.

A man with crinkled leathery skin was fishing at the end of a rickety pontoon and a ferry covered with hundreds of fairy lights was moored at the far end of this inlet.

All of a sudden, the old man started to shout excitedly, at the same time as pulling furiously at his fishing rod. Bit by bit, he was being dragged towards the very end of the pontoon. With a last supreme effort, he hauled his fishing rod out of the sea and wriggling furiously at the end of it was a huge octopus!

"We eat! The old man cried. "We eat supper! I have the supper!"

He did a little dance while bringing in his catch.

Watching this I felt sad. Then suddenly, with a last superlative effort the octopus appeared to jump five feet in the air, cleared the pontoon and landed back into the sea! The old man shouted and screamed and waved his fist at the octopus. Using all eight of his beautiful tentacles, the octopus swiftly swam away.

CHAPTER TWO

'FIDDLER ON THE ROOF'

George looked at him quizzically.

"Kalispera... good evening! Welcome to Thanasis's Taverna," said a voice.

I looked up to see a tall, jolly man carrying a silver tray with a towel draped over his arm.

"What can I get you sir? We close soon but there is still time for some food if you like?"

"I'd like a cold Greek beer, please," said George.

"Excellent. You stay here how long?" He asked.

George replied, "my wife and I are here for nearly three weeks. We have rented a villa at the top of the Olive groves."

"Excellent! Excellent! My name, Thanasis, and this is my taverna. I hope we shall see lots of you. We have wonderful food. All fresh each day. Fish, plenty fish. You will love!"

At this my ears pricked up. Wonderful food! This was my sort of place!

"Woof, woof!" I shouted.

"Quiet," said George. "Mr. Thanasis, I hope you don't mind dogs in your taverna?"

"Mind them! I love them! His name, what you call him?"

"Mr. Thanasis, meet Mr. B... otherwise known as Barnaby."

"I am happy to meet you Barnaby. You are handsome

dog. Now, I go your drinks to get before you die of thirst. I bring Barnaby water with cold ice. I'll be back, two minutes."

With that he vanished inside the old building.

"Do you know what Mr. B?" Said George. "I think we're all going to like it here. Tomorrow we can walk down to this beach. I'll see what Dorothy wants to do. She might like to just sit around the pool in the morning and then come down here for some lunch. Good heavens! What is the man doing?"

Looking towards the taverna I could see Thanasis walking precariously on the rooftop about three meters from the ground. He had a large hammer in his hand and had begun to vigorously hit at a copper pipe that ran from the roof down into the taverna. After several blows and with a satisfied smile on his face he started to carefully descend. He got to the end of the building when his foot slipped, and he tumbled to the ground. Nobody took the slightest notice, so I started squealing and barking. George jumped up and just as he was about to rush to the poor man's aid, Thanasis got up, still clutching his hammer, brushed himself down, and with an enormous smile on his face he went inside the taverna. Two minutes later he appeared, alarmingly balancing a tray with a pitcher of beer above his head.

"I bring your drinks! Excellent! Here is fine beer for you. Here is ice water for Barnaby. You need anything else; you call for Thanasis!"

"Thank you. I saw you fall. Are you alright?"

"Thank you, but I am good. The pipe for beer gets stuck from old cellar so I have to, how you English say, clobber it! Now I must take rubbish to the dustbins. Yamas! Enjoy, yamas!" With that, he was gone!

The taverna had emptied and George was left alone, sipping his beer as I lapped up the glorious cold water. We sat and watched the last of the sun go down. I remember a strange stillness in the air. Not a sound could be heard until suddenly the side door to the kitchen flew open and Thanasis, huffing and puffing, came out pulling a large trolley with several big green plastic sacks on top of it. Humming to himself, he slowly pulled the trolley towards two very large grey metal dustbins that sat on the edge of the beach fifty yards from the front of the taverna. Standing in front of them, he scratched his head then bent to lift up one of the dripping sacks.

With a heave-ho and a grunt, he swung the sack into the dumpster. There was an almighty crashing sound as the glass bottles shattered and hit the bottom of the bin. Looking pleased with himself he went to pick up a second sack, again scratching his head before he did so. This time, as he picked it up, oils, sauces, gravies and other sticky foods dripped onto the hot sand. With one enormous tug he flung the sack into the air, half the contents spilling out around him, before it landed with a thump in the dustbin.

Thanasis gave out a further satisfied grunt and again scratched his head. Heading back towards the taverna he pulled his trousers back up over his large bottom.

"Oh no! We forgot the time. We're late! Dorothy will be furious. Quick, let's go. Sorry Barnaby, I'll tell her it was your fault!"

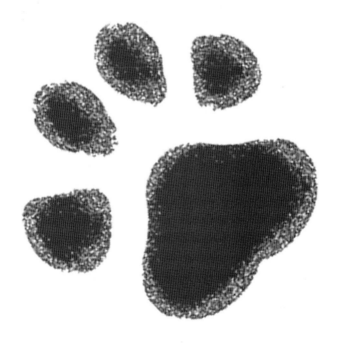

CHAPTER 3

'CATS'

Cats have never really interested me. As a pug dog I have little or nothing in common with cats. At my home in London a cat called Thomas stays with us. He is not ours but for the last two years he seems to have decided to share his living arrangements between ourselves and a family down the road from us. We tolerated each other with a certain indifference and occasionally, just for the fun of it, I have chased him, and he runs squealing up the stairs and hides under a bed. Apart from that we eat different food, play different games and do our best to keep out of each other's way. Occasionally, if I'm bored, I will tease him by watching him stalk a bird. Just as he is about to pounce, I run around him in a yapping frenzy. This alerts the bird who then flies away. The cat, his name is Thomas, will run from me and sit flexing his claws while hissing. It is a silly game but has always helped me to pass a rainy Monday morning. Since I reached the age of three, I have grown out of these silly puppy games and tend to show Thomas how mature and responsible I am now instead.

I tell you all this because it was cats, well kittens, truth be told, that were the cause of my thrilling Greek adventure.

As I sat with George, I looked up and could see he was having a doze. He was still holding onto a glass mug with the last drops of what was now warm beer. It was then I noticed a sudden rapid movement just behind one of the giant dustbins.

As I watched, a tiny ginger kitten appeared slowly from under the wheels of one of the dumpsters. Almost immediately another kitten appeared. This one was also ginger, looking like a twin to the other one.

Carefully, they both crept out from their cover under the large dumpsters, a metal bin full of thrown out food. Looking cautiously around they set about devouring the spilt table scraps, stopping every few seconds to see if anyone was about. Having taken comfort in the knowledge that they were alone, they continued with their feast. Sitting opposite one another, their tails flapping, they lapped up the spillage, putting their paws into the sticky liquid and then licking it off with amazing speed. Looking at them I could only think what fun it would be to join in. George still hadn't finished his beer and was still dozing. I took my chance. Slowly, and very quietly I got up, crossed over the sandy path and walked steadily towards the kittens. They were so busy lapping up the slops that they didn't see me.

"Hello you two!" I said.

I had never seen anyone disappear so quickly, gone! I stood trying to see where they had disappeared to. Nothing! Then I noticed a tiny head with big green eyes peeking out from behind one of the bins. No sooner had it appeared than it was gone.

Just as I was about to return to the table, I saw the same kitten poke his head out again. Only this time it was followed by the second kitten.

"Hello again," I said in a hushed voice. They continued to stare blankly at me. "My name is Barnaby. I'm here on holiday with my 'parents'. What are your names?"

No answer came, they just continued to stare at me without moving.

"I'm very friendly," I told them. "I saw you both playing and thought it would be good fun to join in!" Still nothing.

"Tell me your names. Do you speak English?"

The kittens slowly looked at each other and then replied.

"Yes, we live here, and we can speak English. We speak it because of all the tourists that come here."

"That's wonderful! Tell me your names?"

They went on to tell me that they had not been given

names as two weeks after they were born their mother had been run over by a big lorry. They had been living on their own for nearly ten weeks. At that moment, a great wave of sadness passed over me.

"That's terrible! I am so sorry!"

"I wish we did have a name," the little kitten had said sadly.

"Then you shall," I told them. "Now let me think. I will call you... Anna. As for you my friend, I shall call you... Henry. What do you think?"

The kittens yelped with excitement.

"Etharisto! Etharisto! Thank you!"

"Where do you live?" I asked.

"We live here. It is very nice here. The owner of the taverna is very kind and leaves cool water for us to drink and lets us rummage in these bins," said Henry.

Anna chirped in, "sometimes he leaves us food from the table."

Henry added, "if there is no food we climb up into the dustbins and scavenge around. There is always something to eat in there. It's a lot of fun, most of the time."

There was something in his voice that sent a small shiver down my back. I asked him why he had said 'most of the time'. Little did I know how dangerous that question would prove to be!

CHAPTER FOUR

'BEAUTY AND THE BEAST'

A t that very moment we all heard a long, threatening growl. We looked up and standing proud on top of one of the dumpsters was a large red fox. He looked menacingly towards us, then his glaring eyes rested on me.

"What are you doing, playing with my dinner?"

"Your dinner?" I quizzed. "I don't know what you mean. I haven't been near any of your food!"

"My dinner, you stupid mongrel, are those two!"

A slight panic swept over me.

"Firstly, you big furry-tailed tickling stick, I am not a mongrel. I am a pug dog! Secondly, if you go anywhere near those kittens, you will have me to deal with!"

"That, you ugly little pug, will be my pleasure!"

With that, he leapt off the dumpster and landed one metre in front of me. To say he looked angry would not be doing the word, or the situation, justice.

"My, you're even more ugly than I thought. What is that pathetic curly stump sat on your back?"

Pulling myself up to my full twenty inches I said, "that is my tail!"

"Tail!" He cried, "tail! That's not a tail. This is a tail!"

Slowly he turned his back to show me an enormous bushy tail, of which he was evidently very proud.

"Wow! I see what you mean. That is some tail, let me have a closer look?"

Posturing, he pulled himself up to his full height. I looked quickly to the kittens.

"Run!" I cried.

As I did so I bit into his red bushy tail and held on. He gave out a blood-curdling cry and then ran furiously in a tight circle with me being flung in the air one minute and then hitting the ground the next.

After what seemed like a lifetime, I let go. He sat panting, licking his wound. A quick look and I could see the kittens had fled. The only problem now was how I was going to escape. As I looked back at him, he slowly opened his mouth and flashed the biggest, sharpest teeth I had ever seen.

With a nasty snarl on his face, he shouted at me, "you wretched pug! I'm going to rip your ridiculous head from your pitiful body!" With that, he charged!

CHAPTER FIVE

'CATCH ME IF YOU CAN'

I could feel his hot breath on me as I scampered around to the back of the dumpsters. I could hear him snapping those sharp, yellow, pointed teeth inches behind me. I ran down onto the sand, weaving in and out of the beached boats with him snapping at my tightly curled tail the whole time. I scampered along the beach as fast as my little legs would carry me and then out onto the jetty. Halfway along I stopped to quickly look behind me. There he stood. Hate on his face. Realising that soon I could be his supper I slowly backed up, getting nearer and nearer to the end of the jetty. He followed. Back I went. There were only a few short steps left before the jetty ran out. Then he would catch me and I'd end up being a pug burger! Six steps. He followed. Five steps. He followed. Four steps, Argh! My foot had gone through a small hole in the jetty.

I was stuck. The fox smirked. I pulled and pulled trying to release my foot.

"Not so clever now, pug dog!" He said with a murderous glint in his eye.

It was now or never. With one last pull, scraping all the fur from my leg, I was suddenly free. I still had no way of getting away from him. All I could think of was to jump into the sea, but if I did that my little legs wouldn't get me out again. I was in a bit of a stew, a pug stew! Nearer he came, bigger and bigger.

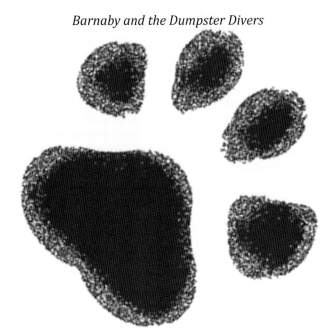

"Well pug," he sneered, "say your prayers, this is the end, for you!"

Two steps. With that he took a giant leap and lunged towards me. I splayed my legs out as far as they would go, and my little belly fell to the decking. I kept my head down with my chin pressed hard to the floor and tightly closed my eyes. The next thing I knew he was flying over my head. Twisting and turning he flew on past the end of jetty and with a big splat, landed in the sea.

Not daring to look back, I shouted, "*sea you again!*"

Then I ran up the jetty onto the beach, past the boats, past the dustbins and back to the table where George was sitting. Fear slowly left me, but I was now totally exhausted after this frightening experience. I sat down next to him trying to catch my breath. George looked down, finished his beer and stood up.

"Come on Mr. B, you lazy thing, it's time to go. You can't lie here all evening. You need some exercise!"

With that, we went home.

CHAPTER SIX

'AIN'T MISBEHAVING'

It turned out that Thanasis was a rogue, but a rogue in the nicest way. Over the next few days, after lying in the sun followed by joyful splashes in the pool, we would all go down to the taverna for a late lunch. At first, I was fearful of meeting the fox again, but thankfully he was never to return. We would walk down the stony path that had large nets lying under the trees in order to catch the olives and head towards the little cove. As we went, I would get more and more excited. I knew that once we reached the taverna and found our table, the fun would begin. Thanasis would wave his white napkin at us as he crossed to our table.

"Kherete! Welcome! You want drink? The day is hot, you need good, Greek beer. I get for you!"

Each day after ordering cold beer, my parents would carefully study the menu and after great deliberation always ordered the mezze, an assortment of small, Greek dishes.

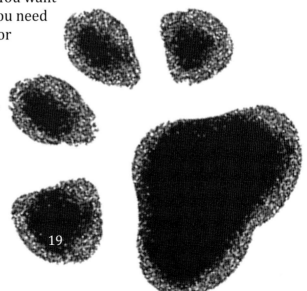

"Mezze, of course! I recommend…"

"Thanasis we don't want a lot. Just a small snack for lunch."

"But of course! Let me recommend for you… leave all to me!"

With that he had gone. Twenty minutes later he would return with an enormous tray balanced on his wide shoulders.

"See my friends, see what I have for you today!"

With that, the tray was lowered to the table and the talking would begin.

"Special for you! Loukanika, spicy farm sausages. Then I have, made fresh this morning, these Saganaki, delicious fried hard cheese. Here a special plate of Taramosalata with some zucchini fritters. Then we have…"

"Wait," shouted George, "we said a light lunch!"

"But this is a light lunch! Now, here we have some Keftedes, how you say, meatballs, and then for the last we have some Tzatziki with pitta bread. Enjoy! Enjoy! I fetch you more beer," again, he was gone.

"Well," said Dorothy, "I'd hate to see what a large meal looks like, we'll never get through all this!"

This is where I would come in. "Woof! I'm here, don't forget about me!"

"Oh George, look at Barnaby. I wonder what he's saying?"

Looking at George, I barked again.

What am I saying? What am I saying? I'm saying, what are you eating and where's mine?

"George, I think he wants a little bit of our mezze… is that right Barnaby? Would you like a little bit of sausage?"

"Woof, woof! Woof! Yes! Sausage, and don't forget the meatballs… they look good too!"

To make sure of sharing the feast I'd run round and round the wonky table, yapping as I went, while the 'Parents' would laugh and tell each other how cute I was.

"Cute?" said my father. "He's misbehaving!"

That is when I'd suddenly stop and sit in front of George, wag my tail and look up at him with big, doleful eyes as if to say I'm not misbehaving! I am cute!

"Look Dorothy, he's sat down. Here you go Barnaby, a nice piece of sausage."

This little ritual would continue for half an hour while they ate. At the end of our lunch, I'd sit next to George while they both drank their beers. Looking over to the dustbins, I could see the kittens keeping out of the sun as they slept in their shadow. Thanasis would again take the scraps to the bins. As soon as he had filled the bins and returned to the taverna the kittens would jump up onto the lids, check around to make sure all was clear and then dive in. They would disappear for ten minutes at a time and then suddenly appear, as if coming up for air only to dive back in and disappear again seconds later. Yes, they were true dustbin divers.

As the days passed 'The Parents' would read books or listen to their iPods while I would sit by the pool dipping in and out of the shade. Occasionally, I'd jump up onto the wall that surrounded the pool terrace to see if the kittens could be seen. It appeared that they slept hidden from the sun most of the day. I kept an eye out for the fox but thankfully he seemed to have disappeared for good, with his bitten tail firmly between his legs!

Each morning Maria, a large lady with long, jet-black hair and the rosiest cheeks I'd ever seen, would arrive to clean the villa. She would start in the kitchen first and then continue onto the lounge. The bedrooms were always left until last just in case 'The Parents' were still in bed.

As she washed pots, swept floors and made beds she would sing loudly along to the music being played on the radio.

It amused me that when she sang, she always got the words wrong! Once she had finished cleaning the bedroom, she would move outside to the patio area of the villa. At this I would quickly go and hide, but always to no avail. She would hunt me down and when found, picked me up and squeeze the life out of me.

"Barnaby! My little friend, you handsome doggie!"

Then she would start to pinch my cheeks followed by a pulling of my ears and a smothering of kisses. No matter how much I wriggled to get away, her large arms and ample body would hold me in a vice like grip.

"Look!" She would shout, "he loves me! Barnaby loves his Maria!"

After what seemed like an eternity, she would put me down and I would run squealing to find George and try to hide until she had gone.

Maria would leave with a thousand goodbyes which continued until she was halfway down the hillside and out of sight.

Dorothy exclaimed to George, "you really should do something about Maria with Barnaby. It's not fair. The poor little chap is scared of her!"

"She doesn't mean any harm," said George. "Barnaby needs to be more friendly. He seems to lack a little of my passion and enthusiasm!"

"What!" I thought. "A lack of passion and enthusiasm! He should see me alone with a Big Mac!"

We had been at the villa for over a week. The weather was fantastic, and the food seemed never ending.

Each morning before the sun rose, I'd sit by the pool and look down the hillside to the dustbins. I'd watch to see that the kittens were alright, and no harm had come to them. They would run and chase each other, playing topsy turvy until the sun was fully up and then they would decide it was time to eat. The two of them would scrabble up the giant dustbins and dive in for their morning breakfast. This was a daily ritual. Not only were Henry and Anna the most delightful kittens, but by now had become my friends.

CHAPTER SEVEN

'A BED-FULL OF FOREIGNERS'

Friday night was hot and humid. The air was stifling and uncomfortable. Laying on the bed, as I always did, between 'The Parents' I was getting little sleep. They both tossed and turned throughout the night. What little sleep I did get was constantly being disturbed. Eventually I couldn't take it anymore and I decided the only thing to do, was to get up. I jumped off the bed very quietly and wandered into the lounge. I sat staring out of the large window. The room was hot and stuffy, I was desperate to get some air... and there it was! A small window at the side of the enormous glass wall, and it was half open. A gateway to a little breeze, a gentle wind.

I jumped up on the sofa, scrambled along the back of it and climbed onto the windowsill, at the same time knocking down a glass vase that contained an orchid. Whoops! That was going to mean trouble when 'The Parents' got up in the morning!

I peered out of the window and taking a deep breath, squeezed myself out and landed on the tough prickly grass below. I checked myself over for any broken paws. Deciding that all was well, I plodded over to the pool.

Jumping up on the surrounding wall I sat on my tail as I relished the cool breeze.

Finding a towel that had been left out I snuggled down, creating a makeshift bed, and was, at last, able to sleep.

Dreaming peacefully about Lilly's Kitchen, a rather splendid food shop for pugs and other hounds, I awoke with a start. 'Ouch!' I heard myself say. What was happening? 'Ouch again!' I thought. That hurt! I had been bitten.

I jumped up from my makeshift bed as yet again something chomped at me. I realised I was in a bed full of foreigners. Red ants! The towel was swarming with little red ants. I jumped off the towel and realised that I too was covered with them. 'Ouch! Ouch!' I was being bitten alive!

I ran round in a circle, barking as loud as I could, trying to fling them off, but to no avail. What should I do? There was only one thing for it, I leapt from the wall and landed with a big splash in the pool. Oh, the relief! But that relief was to be short lived!

My little paws flapped around in the water and slowly I managed to get to the pool's edge. Ok, breathe slowly and keep calm. One of the more endearing things about a pug dog is their legs, or to be more accurate, the lack of them. It was all very well jumping into the pool but an entirely different matter to get out of it. I clambered around the edges trying to find a way to scramble my way out.

The pool ladder was no good, my legs were just too small. This was not looking good. Time to wake 'The Parents'. I barked and barked. Nothing! I howled and howled. Still nothing! My legs were getting tired and any strength in my little body was quickly turning to weakness. I could feel myself starting to sink. No! Fight, fight with all my might. Bark, howl, yap, anything to get help. Nothing.

This was not the time for my 'Parents' to have fallen asleep! My legs had all but given up as my little body got heavier and heavier. Slowly, very slowly, I was sinking, now for the second time. Was this it? Was this the end?

With one last huge effort my front paws caught onto the top rung of the pool ladder. Fighting for a grip I pulled myself halfway out of the water. My paws clung on and I gradually hauled another inch of me from these now-threatening waters. Exhausted, I took one more deep breath and with a final effort pulled myself almost to safety. Holding on to get my breath back for a final push.

I felt something strange.

No! Please not this! I looked at my left paw. There it was a red ant... and it was huge! It was crawling between my toes. Suddenly he bit me, puncturing my paw with his sting.

I instantly let go and fell backwards into the pool.

So, this was it, this was the unhappy end!

I had no strength left. I was slowly sinking into the salty pool water. I struggled up for air one last time but down I went again. I began to lose consciousness.

Just as I had resigned myself to my fate a hand suddenly appeared from above, grabbed me by the scruff of the neck and pulled me to safety.

"George, is he alright?" I heard my mother sob.

"I think so. Poor little chap. Can you get me a couple of dry towels? We need to dry him off."

"George, how did this happen? Why were you asleep! It's all your fault! I'll never forgive you... I'll... I'll... I'll go and get the towels," and she hurried off.

"Well Barnaby, I'm not sure how this is all my fault. That was a silly thing to do. You nearly drowned. You mad little pug dog. What were you thinking?"

"George," shouted Dorothy as she ran from the lounge clutching several towels, "how is he? Will he be alright?"

"Yes," said George. "He's looking better. Let me have those."

Taking the towels, he began to dry me off and slowly, I began to revive. Although shaken, I realised that this wonderful man who was now drying me off, was my 'dad' and that he had saved my life. Finding renewed energy, I jumped up, wagged my tail and licked every square inch of his face.

"George, I'll just get him some fresh water, he needs a cold drink and then perhaps a little food," said Dorothy.

I was quite dry now and was being expertly cuddled. Dorothy soon returned with a bowl of cold water and a small dish of minced meat swimming in doggie gravy, yummy!

For the next hour or two I was pampered, petted and spoilt by the two people I loved most in this world.

After all the drama and having checked I was alright for the seventh time, 'The Parents' made themselves cups of tea and coffee. They decided they would catch up with their broken sleep by lying by the pool. I suspected that it was also a way of keeping an eye on me. They had found me a clean towel which they made into a little bed and Dorothy had put it next to George along with a biscuit for me to nibble on.

What a day, I thought. It was still only eight o'clock in the morning and yet so much had happened. I looked at my paw that had been gnawed by the ant. It was still painful, but at least I was alive.

I gave my bitten paw a few of my best licks as I peered out to the sea. The sun was now high in the sky, the sea was calm, and the beach had started to come alive with tourists claiming their place. My eyes wandered from the beach and over towards the taverna. I could see the two dustbins spilling over with slops from the previous night. From around the back of the bins I saw the two kittens appear. Henry and Anna were jumbling around, occasionally checking if anyone could see them.

The kittens, having decided no one was about and that their breakfast was calling, climbed up onto the top of these metal dumpsters, squeezed themselves under the ill-fitting lids and disappeared inside to enjoy a morning feast. A small van pulled up outside of the taverna and Thanasis got out with a large wooden box of newly picked vegetables along with a box of fresh fish and assorted meats. Finally, he fetched a large basket tray, full of fresh rolls and olive breads.

A feeling of love and contentment filled my heart. Little did I know that this feeling would be ripped away from me and my real Greek adventure was just about to begin.

CHAPTER EIGHT

'THE INCREDIBLE JOURNEY'

Having unloaded his van Thanasis disappeared into the kitchen. The taverna had not yet opened and all was quiet.

A very small Greek lady, dressed all in black and carrying a silver and pink walking stick, passed the taverna and carried on until she got onto the sandy beach. As she went, she threw pieces of stale bread towards the seagulls who, in turn, swooped down and grabbed at it greedily.

Looking further along the beach a large ferry called 'The Heather Mary' was being prepared in order to carry eager tourists along to the beautiful bays. It would take them in and out of small lagoons mooring by rocky beaches where they could dive and picnic. You could see market workers loading the vessel with melons, green peppers, onions, cucumbers, olives and the best tomatoes in the world. Once the delivery was complete they would scurry off and drive to the next marina to offload their wares onto the other ferries. Next to be loaded onto The Heather Mary were different wines and beers. These were delivered by several jolly merchants, who thought it a good idea to taste their wines as they boarded it onto the ferry. Having taken all this in, I glanced back at the dumpsters. Henry and Anna had yet to emerge from their takeaway, they had obviously found some tasty nibbles inside these dustbins.

Thinking about them, I realised I had become very fond of these two adorable kittens.

'The Parents' were still sunbathing by the pool. I closed my eyes and thought of how lucky I had been. Suddenly, a horrible clatter came from below the villa. It was far in the distance, but the hullabaloo was getting louder and louder. From out of nowhere came this enormous truck, looking every inch like a monster

from a Disney film. It nuzzled up alongside the two giant metal dustbins and then squealed to a halt, breathing out a massive hiss with blue smoke emerging from all sides of its giant body. The back of it snorted and groaned, and it appeared to open what you could mistake to be a giant mouth. To my horror it started to pick up the two dustbins and lifted them high into the air! It gave out another loud rumble, followed by a piercing hiss, then it slowly lowered both of the bins down into its belly and seemingly 'gobbled' the contents. At the same time, it bellowed out a loud crunching sound. The contents of the bins! My friends, Henry and Anna were in there!

Just as I had realised this, the monster truck plucked the bins from out its belly, raised them again into the air and placed them down onto the sand with a crash.

I looked frantically to see if I could spot the two kittens. They were nowhere to be seen! With what sounded like a loud snarl or growl, the truck started off along the beach road. No! The kittens must still be inside this monster. Had it eaten Henry and Anna?

As I was trying to think what I could do, my 'mother' woke.

"George," she said, "what was that terrible noise? It's woken me up!"

"Nothing to worry about Darling, it's only the rubbish men collecting from Thanasis's taverna."

"Well George, it's very noisy, it gave me quite a start!"

"It sounds as if they might have finished," said George.

He got up and to have a look.

"I don't think we'll hear it again. They only pick up once every two weeks. There's nowhere on the island to put the rubbish so they take it by barge to the mainland."

Take it by barge to the mainland! No! The kittens! My friends! What could I do? I had to save them. Jumping up I barked as loud as my lungs would let me.

"Dorothy, what's wrong with Barnaby?"

Dorothy picked me up. "I don't think he's been well since he nearly drowned in your pool. What's wrong little chap?"

I jumped free and ran around in frantic circles, stopping to look back at them, and then at the disappearing truck. It was obvious they hadn't a clue as to what I was trying to tell them.

"He doesn't seem to like that rubbish truck," said George.

Not like the rubbish truck! Not like it! How would you feel? It has just swallowed my two best friends!

I realised there was no way I was going make either of them understand my plight. I had to save the kittens.

I knew then what I had to do. With a tear in my eye, I jumped up and gave them both a pug licky-kiss and one last adoring glance, then I jumped over the wall, clambered down the hillside and ran after this 'monster' as fast as my ant-chomped paw could take me.

Where I was going, and what I was going to do, I had no idea. What I did know was this was the start of a very scary and dangerous adventure. I thought of the two kittens.

Hang on, I thought. Hang on! I'm coming! I'm coming!

CHAPTER NINE

'RATATOUILLE'

I ran down the steep slope of the olive groves desperately trying to see where that dumpster monster had gone but by the time I had got to the taverna it had disappeared! Which way to go? I ran out towards the beach and then up to the sandy road, but there was no sign of it. I sat for a minute to get my breath, thinking... thinking. It was then I remembered that George had said they took the rubbish down to the port and then loaded it onto barges. So, the port it must be! The only problem was that I hadn't a clue as to where the port lay. Ok, obviously the port had to be down by the sea. Simples! If I could cut across the olive groves and find the port, I might be able to get there before the dumpster truck. Once there, I could wait for the dumpster and, somehow, rescue the kittens. Easy peasy!

I ran as fast as I could to the top of the hillside and along the dusty paths, crossing back down into the valley of olive groves. There were hundreds of olive trees, all with nets laying around them on the ground, waiting to catch the olives as they fell.

This made it very difficult to cross the valley as I kept getting my paws stuck in the web of netting.

More of a problem was that I wasn't sure if I was even going in the right direction. Mile after mile I ran, until I found myself on the edge of a little village. Where now? I stood trying to decide when I heard a voice shouting behind me.

"Wot are you doing in my village, Ugly?"

I didn't look round as I thought he couldn't be talking to me. No one would call me ugly!

"Oi, I'm talking to you, Ugly."

It appeared he was talking to me!

Turning slowly, I saw the biggest rat I have ever seen. Either side of him were two equally big rats. To say they didn't look friendly was an understatement!

"I'm sorry. My name is Barnaby, not Ugly. I had no idea you were talking to me!"

"Listen to him! 'I had no idea you were talking to me!' Well, Mr. La-di-la I was talking to you. Me mates 'ere want to know wot you're doing here!"

"May I say you speak very good English."

"That's because I'm English mate! I'm known as Reggie the Rat. We come over 'ere on the cruise ships from Southampton for the summer. There are rich pickings 'ere if you know where to go and wot you're doing. Now, before we rough you up, I'll ask you again, wot you doing 'ere?"

Picking myself up to my full half-metre height I replied, "well, if you must know I am trying to save the lives of my two best friends. You are delaying me from doing this!"

"You're a plucky little brat, I'll give you that," he said. "Who are these so-called friends?"

"Two little kittens called Henry and Anna that live by the old Agni taverna."

"Kittens!" He roared. "Kittens, we can't stand kitties can we lads? We eat kitties don't we lads?"

The two nodded while at the same time giving out a loud belch.

"Well, you'll not be eating these kittens," I answered back.

As I said this, I noticed that the other two rats had crept to either side of me. I was surrounded!

"I don't think you understand who you're yakking to!"

Squeaked one of the other rats. "This is Reggie the Rat, the most 'orrible rat to ever live in London's east end."

With that Reggie shouted to them, "let's get 'im lads!"

Before I knew what was happening, the other two jumped onto my back, trying to bite into my neck, while Reggie ran straight at me attacking my front paw. I tried to break away, but I didn't have the strength to throw them off me. This was not good. If I didn't do something soon, I'd be a dish of ratatouille! I kept running in circles trying to fling them off in any direction. I juggle-struggled, rolling over on my back, snapping at their tails, but they just hung on. The pain in my neck was now considerable and I began to feel a little faint.

Suddenly, everything stopped! All went quiet. The two rats climbed off of my back. Reggie stopped moving and seemed to be staring into space. The other two joined him and all three of them slowly started to back away.

Carefully, I stood up and looked around me. What was going on? Then I saw him, it was as if the sheriff had come to town!

35

CHAPTER TEN

'MOODYWARP THE MOLE'

Leave the pug alone!" He said in an Anglo-Greek accent.

"Leave that little pug alone!"

Nobody moved. Several metres away from us was a velvety grey-black furry creature with a short tail, tiny eyes, and a pink pointed snout, standing about six inches high. Then I noticed, he was wearing... glasses! Who, or what, was this?

"Listen mate," said Reggie, "butt out. This is my village and my fight. Keep your snout out of my business or me and the lads will 'ave to teach you a lesson."

The rats stood staring at each other, slightly trembling, without a word being said. After a couple of minutes, Reggie the Rat slowly started to move towards this odd, and unexpected, little hero.

"That's far enough! My name is Moodywarp... Moodywarp the Mole. Now why don't you be good little rats and go home?"

"Moodywarp the Mole! Well, Mr. Moodywarp my name is Reggie the Rat and if anyone is going home it's you, my tubby little rodent. So, get going!"

"Oh dear!" Said Moody. "I had hoped you'd see a little sense. Pug, you stay where you are while I take care of these... gentlemen."

The three rats laughed loudly while at the same time they took several menacing paces towards Moodywarp.

"Now listen boys," said Moodywarp. "Why don't we just be friends. I don't want any trouble. This nice little fella with his funny curly tail, he doesn't want any trouble, do you pug?"

"No," I quickly stammered.

"Tough!" The rat countered.

Moodywarp slowly removed his spectacles and carefully folded the arms. He then placed them in his pocket.

"Last chance guys," said Moodywarp forcefully. "No one wants trouble. Let's be cool. Just go home."

"Well Tubby, it's like this. You don't want trouble, but we love trouble! Don't we boys? Get him!"

Moodywarp shouted again for me to stay put and do nothing. The three rats suddenly all rushed at Moody. One ran to the left of him and one to the right. Reggie ran straight at him. Moodywarp dived to his left and at the same time did an ariel summersault and jumped over his attacker. The second rat rushed so hard towards Moodywarp that he couldn't stop, and in doing so smashed head-on into the other rat, first knocking him over and then landing with a thump on top of him.

Moodywarp, taking his chance, jumped on top of the two rats, stamping with his powerful feet on their backs several times. Just before jumping off, he flashed his two enormous front teeth and bit them both on their bottoms! Both dazed, and with cries of pain, they staggered to their feet and holding their posteriors, ran off. Throughout this Reggie had stopped in his tracks.

"Come back here," he shouted. "Come back here you lily-livered rats!" But it was too late. They had gone.

Reggie turned back to Moodywarp with an evil snarl on his face.

"I guess it's just you and me," he said.

Moody, checked to make sure the others had really gone, replied "it doesn't have to be this way. Go and find your friends, leave us alone and let's forget all about this."

"In your dreams!" Reggie snarled moving closer to him. When he was but a metre from him, Moodywarp held up his right paw. Click! Six sharp claws shot out. He then held up his left paw. Click. Another six sharp claws appeared. I couldn't believe my eyes! Moodywarp had six claws on each paw! Reggie took a step back but stood his ground. Breathing quickly, he took a tentative step towards Moodywarp.

As he got close, Moodywarp opened his mouth and flashed two of the biggest, sharpest, yellowest set of front teeth I had ever seen! Reggie, not sure if this was such a good idea after all, turned and started to walk away. Moodywarp watched him go. Thinking it was now safe, he turned back to me. No sooner had he turned his back than Reggie came running at him and taking a sudden lunge at Moodywarp, tried desperately to bite his neck. Moodywarp dived to one side and the rat fell to the ground and landed upside down next to him. As he was about to get up Moodywarp trod on his tail, trapping it. With his left paw, claws out, he picked up the rat's tail and with his sharp, yellow two front teeth took a big bite out of it! Reggie screamed and decided it was time to run. As he pulled away, his long tail dislodged from Moodywarps' mouth and he flew up into the air. A loud squeal could be heard throughout the village. With his tail now firmly between his legs, Reggie the Rat ran as far and as fast as he could.

"He'll have to do some shopping tomorrow," said Moodywarp with a smile, "he'll need a little *retail* therapy!"

CHAPTER ELEVEN

'LES MISÉRABLES!'

The sound of sobbing could be heard from the villa bedroom as George paced up and down along the patio. He thought he'd never be able to comfort his wife again.

He walked through to the kitchen and made a cup of tea which he took to Dorothy. He gently woke her from her half sleep.

"Here you are darling, a nice cup of tea."

She turned over and looked up at him. "I don't want tea! I want Barnaby safely back home."

George gulped and promptly dropped the cup of tea in shock.

"Dorothy! What have you done... your head, it's all bleeding!"

"What? what are you talking about?"

"You've got blood all over you head!"

Dorothy jumped up from the bed and ran to the bathroom. George ran in after her.

"Are you alright? How has this happened?" He said with panic in his voice. "I'm going to call a doctor," he went to get his phone.

"George... George! It's alright, look!" She ran her hand through her hair and over her face and then licked her fingers.

"What are you doing?" He asked with panic in his voice.

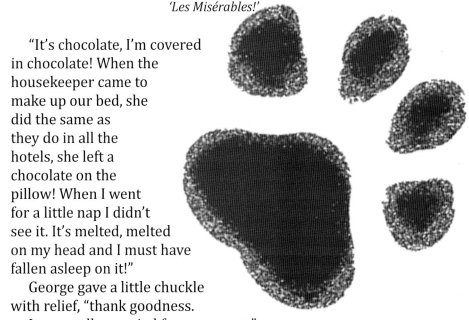

'Les Misérables!'

"It's chocolate, I'm covered
in chocolate! When the
housekeeper came to
make up our bed, she
did the same as
they do in all the
hotels, she left a
chocolate on the
pillow! When I went
for a little nap I didn't
see it. It's melted, melted
on my head and I must have
fallen asleep on it!"

George gave a little chuckle
with relief, "thank goodness.
I was really worried for a moment."

"Apart from being very upset, I'm
fine George. What are we going to do
about Barnaby? We leave here in four days. Will we ever find
him?"

"I'm sure we will. The local police are looking for him and I'm
going out again in a minute to look along the surrounding olive
groves. We'll find him I'm sure."

"Oh George, if we don't get him back, I know I'll never be
happy again. I don't think I have ever been this miserable. It's
been nearly two days now, there's been no sign of him. Poor
little chap, he must be so frightened and hungry. Four days
George, four days! That's all the time we have to find him."

"Cheer up darling, it will all work out I promise."

"Cheer up? I've nothing to cheer up about! I've never been
so miserable and I'm sure Barnaby will be even more unhappy.
This whole holiday is... miserable!"

With that, she ran out onto the patio, sat on the edge of a sun
lounger and cried.

CHAPTER TWELVE

'THE COMEDY OF ERRORS'

Reggie the rat had gone, and we could at last relax a little.

"That was good fun!" Said Moodywarp. "Now tell me, what you are doing roaming around the streets of Corfu, all on your own?"

"It's a long story!" I replied.

"In that case you had better start at the beginning. Let's begin with your name."

"I'm called Barnaby, I come from England and I'm on holiday here with my 'Parents.'"

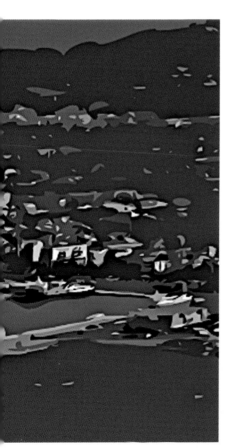

"They can't be very good parents if they allow you out on your own?"

"Oh, but they are! They are the best! This is all my fault, you see I've... I've sort of... runaway!"

"Run away! But why?"

I took a very long deep breath and then blurted out to him all that had happened.

"It's a long story. I'm staying at a villa up in the hills and looking down each morning I could see this taverna sat in a little cove, and each morning I could see two kittens appear on the beach and dive into two dumpsters sat along from outside the taverna and they would eat and play... and we became friends and then, one morning a big dumpster truck came along and put the two big dustbins into its belly and gobbled up the rubbish along with the kittens and then it drove off! When I saw this, I knew I had to rescue them, I jumped down from the villa and was trying to find the dumpster truck when I encountered those rotten rats. Then you came along and saved me. That's about it!" I took another deep breath.

"That's quite a story! So, what are you planning to do now?"

"I'm not sure, but I think that dumpster monster is heading towards the port along the docks. The trouble is I've no idea where that is."

I also explained that I was worried that even if I managed to catch up with the truck, I didn't think my legs would be long enough to climb into it and look for the kittens. Finally, and most importantly, I explained that from tomorrow I would only have three days left before I had to be back at the villa as 'The Parents' would be driving home on Sunday. If I didn't get back by then I would be stranded on my own in Corfu, possibly forever!

Moodywarp chirped up, "this all sounds a bit like a comedy of errors. Especially dealing with those ridiculous rats. Barnaby, I know you have done your very best, but I fear your planning has not been too good."

A little taken aback and upset, I blurted, "thank you very much for all your help. I won't bother you anymore. I'll be on my way."

"Wait a minute! Don't get the hump! I think you are a very brave pug dog. However, now you need a little help, and a plan, if you are going to rescue those kittens."

"I don't have anyone to help me," I whimpered.

"You do now," he said placing his glasses back onto the edge of his nose. "I'll help you. Now our first priority is to get to the port. By the way, I should tell you, you were, in fact, going in the wrong direction. The port is the other way! Never mind that, we need to get going, but in the right direction! Come along!"

With that, he set off. I gathered myself together and chased after him. As we ran along, he told me that he lived in Kassiopi. He loved tunnelling under the olive trees, and he was proud that there was hardly a local farmer that he hadn't upset! I asked Moodywarp about his glasses. He told me that all moles have very bad eyesight because most of their life is spent tunnelling underground in the dark. I asked him why and he said he hadn't a clue, burrowing just came naturally and all moles did it. It turned out that one day, while he was burrowing under a particularly juicy grapevine, he found the lens from a pair of broken glasses that had probably belonged to an old farmhand. He took one of the lenses back to his home and then, with his sharp teeth, split it into four pieces. He then found an old wire coat hanger and chewed a piece off to make a frame for the lenses. He took two of the small glass pieces and made his own pair of spectacles.

His best friend was a hedgehog call Horace. Horace had broken one of his legs and so with the remaining wire from the coat hanger Moodywarp had made him a little stick with a handle that hooked around his neck to keep him steady. It had become very obvious that this was a highly inventive mole.

As we carried on walking, he told me of all the adventures he had been involved in. Halfway through one of his wonderful stories he stopped abruptly. Shouting, with laughter in his voice, he pointed furiously.

"Look over there, we've made it. Those, my friend, are the docks!"

CHAPTER THIRTEEN

'SHOW BOAT'

Looking down from the cliff top there, in all its splendour, sat the magnificent docks of Kerkira.

"Moodywarp, you are wonderful!

I may never have found this on my own. How can I ever thank you?"

"You don't have to thank friends, not true friends. That is what we are now, true friends."

"We sure are," I replied. "What's more I want you to visit me in England and we will... Moodywarp, look!"

There it was, the monster dumpster truck, parked dockside near to an old hut with massive, coiled ropes alongside it. Moored next to this was a very long barge, about fifty metres in length.

Twenty or so men were trudging all over it, pulling up ropes, starting engines and stacking crates containing fruit and vegetables.

I could see four men off-loading several dustbin containers from the barge, all of which appeared empty. The rubbish must have already been off-loaded into the hold of the barge. That meant the kittens were probably trapped in the hold!

"Moodywarp," I cried. "The kittens must be on board, that's the dumpster! It's leaving. We must get down there now!"

As I said this, a loud horn blasted from the barge. The flag that was fixed on a long pole at the back of the vessel was now being taken down. The sound of engines had burst into life.

"Come on! The barge is leaving, I must get onto it!"

"Follow me!" With that, Moodywarp took off like a rocket. I follow as fast as I could. On we went, down the hills, skipping over fallen olive branches and tripping over nets and small rocks that were half buried in the ground. Finally, we got to the outer edge of the dockside.

"Made it! We've made it!" I shouted with relief.

Relief that was soon over. The barge had just started to move off. I'd missed it after all! Moodywarp looked sad and disheartened.

"I'm sorry Barnaby. We got here just too late."

I wasn't going to give up after all we had been through.

"Moody, thank you for everything, you're a great and brave friend, but I can't give up now."

"But what can you do?" He asked.

"There might just be a way!" I shouted back at him and I started to run towards the moving barge.

I had about one hundred metres to cover to get to the barge. I ran and ran, sixty metres away, but the barge was moving further away from the dockside. On I ran, twenty meters from the barge, ten metres and then two meters from the edge of the dockside. The barge was hovering just a metre from the dock. It was now or never. I ran on and as I got to the dockside wall, without stopping, I took a long flying leap into the air. Keeping the flagpole in my sight, I flew through the air and reached the flagpole. I wrapped my curly tail around it and in a spiral motion slid down to the bottom, landing with a bump on the deck. A little dazed, I looked about me. Further along the barge were several of the crew pulling in the ropes and curling them into neat piles. No one, it appeared, had seen me. I looked out towards the dockside to see if I could spot Moody, but he was nowhere to be seen. I was now on my own.

On my own yes, but I was on the barge. I had to start looking for my friends and despite everything, I had a chance of saving them. That was, of course, if my two best friends were still alive!

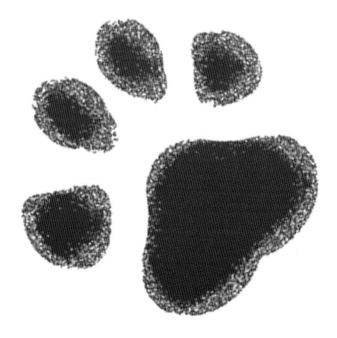

CHAPTER FOURTEEN

'WAIT UNTIL DARK'

Hiding between several large rusting chains and hooks that were attached to an enormous crane, I kept very still. Slowly the barge left the harbour and headed towards Greece's mainland. I had no idea how long this journey would take. I knew I had to find the kittens as quickly as possible then, somehow, get us all off the boat and to safety. Where could they be? The sun was beginning to set and soon it would be dark. I decided that discretion would be the better part of valour and I would wait until it was dark before starting my search. I hid under an old tarpaulin sheet covering one of the lifeboats and waited.

An hour passed and we headed further and further out to sea. The general hubbub and chatter from the crew died down and slowly, one by, one the men left the deck. Still, I waited. A further half hour came and went before I dared peek out from under the tarpaulin. There was nobody to be seen. I left the safety of the lifeboat and slowly padded along the deck. Past the stabilising castings towards the stern, past the towing points and pass the navigation lights. As I got further along the barge, I could hear music and laughter coming from a large canteen room where all the men were enjoying their supper. Slowly, I crept under the porthole-shaped windows and along to the steel steps that descended into the bowels of the boat. Down I went. At the bottom of these steps was a long corridor. Looking along this corridor I could see thick hanging curtains posing as doors into each of the cabins.

I needed to check each one to see if my two friends had managed to escape and were hiding in any of them. Entering the first cabin I saw it contained hundreds of boxes of tinned food, it was a sort of pantry. I moved along to the next one. This contained tray after tray of different sorts of vegetables. Onto the next. As soon as I crawled under this thick curtain I knew where I was. The pungent smell told my little squashed pug nose that I had entered into the men's toilet! I quickly got my little wiggly bottom out of there and then wondered what to do next.

I heard two men outside. Quickly I ran behind an evil smelling bin. One of the men went for a piddle while the other washed his hands at the dirty sink.

"Another couple of hours and we'll be docking in Igoumenitsa," said the taller of the two.

"This is last time this vessel sails... they scrap it."

"I heard," the other one replied, "after we dock, it goes to scrap yard to be broken up... they will crush it!"

"Can't be soon enough," said the other.

Then, they were gone.

CHAPTER FIFTEEN

'GREASE'

C rush it! Not with my friends on board! I carried on to the next cabin and crawled under the tatty curtain door.

Well, this was a surprise! As I looked around, I saw a room painted entirely in white. There was a wooden bed with a huge bulbus lump under a white duvet. Next to it was a white bedside table with a small lamp with a white shade on it. On the wall to the left of the bed hung several white jackets with matching white trousers. They were all covered in grease and other stains. Whoever lived in this room liked white, but not enough to clean the grease off the white jackets! Being satisfied there were no kittens I was just about to leave when I thought I'd have a final check under the bed. As I approached, the bed started to creak, a huge groan came from under the duvet and an enormous man with long pigtail hair and a small round cap on his head emerged. In his hand was an empty ouzo bottle. He sat up and gave a gigantic burp, then looking around, half awake, his bloodshot eyes landed on me. Scary! Quickly, I dived under the bed with the vague hope he would think he was having a bad dream. All was quiet, nothing stirred. My heart raced. Maybe he hadn't seen me after all?

"Giant rat! Help!" He shouted out at the top of his voice.

"Rat! Big! A giant!" He again cried out.

'Grease'

Two men came running into the cabin, all shouting at the same time.

"Mister Wong what's the matter?"

"Mister Wight, I see large rat with curled up noodle on his back!"

Noodle on my back? Just a minute! that's my beautiful tail!

"Mister Wong, you had bad dream, there's nothing here.

I think Chef, you been drinking again! You see things!"

That explained all the white clothing... this Mister Wong was the ship's chef.

"I no see things! I see giant rat with eyes that bulge!"

Despite lying in fear under the bed I was pretty annoyed at being called a giant rat with bulging eyes.

"So, Mister Wong where is this super rodent?" Asked Mister Wight.

"He ran from me... I think maybe he hide under bed."

My heart was racing, I was trapped. Any minute I could be caught. Why had I got myself into this scrape? I couldn't see much under the bed as it was dark and very dusty. I felt around and put my left paw into a rather smelly liquid. It was only later I realised that it was poo! I Crawled to the edge of the bed checking for an escape route. There wasn't one!

"Mister Wong," said Mister Wight, "I show you, there's no rat under bed with a noodle on his back!"

Suddenly, a large grappling hook appeared. It started to sweep back and forth frantically searching under the bed!

CHAPTER SIXTEEN

'WICKED'

I squatted under the bed without moving as the grappling hook got nearer and nearer to me. Slowly, I slid from the bottom back to the top as the hook continued its search. Escape looked impossible. The only option was to make a run for it. Stored under this bed I found an old plastic mooring buoy. With all my strength I kicked it with my back legs. It shot out on the left side of the bed.

"There!" Cried Mister Wong. "Get him! Get him!"

All three ran round to the other side of bed to find 'the rat'.

"Mister Wong! This is no rat this is a ship's buoy!"

I ran out from the bottom of the bed and made my escape.

"Mister Wight... look! There he goes! I was right and you were wrong!" With that, they chased after me.

I ran past several cabins and then dived through an open door and into a large room. Looking round for somewhere to hide, I saw that I was in the ship's kitchen. There was an old cooker with big saucepans with dirty lids sitting on the top of it. A kettle was whistling, and a dishwasher was whirring loudly. In the corner was a stack of old wooden crates. I squeezed behind them, tucked in my tail and lay there in silence. No sooner had I done so when the two chefs and another man came bursting into the room.

"Mister Wight, you look over there, Mr. Choo you look in that cupboard, while I look over here."

"No rat in cupboard," shouted Mr. Choo.

"Rat no here," echoed Mister Wight.

Mister Wong, looking behind the boxes, shouted loudly, "lookie... it's the rat! I told you!"

I pushed my way out from behind the boxes, dashed past the chef, past Mister Wight and Mr. Choo, and had just got to the entrance when a large lobster creel flew above me and then landed on top of me. Trying desperately to get out from under it, I realised it was impossible. The lobster creel was a large box shape, made of steel, rope and braided netting.

"I got him. I got the rat," cried the chef.

"Well done Mister Wong, you a very clever... no you not clever... this no rat. This is pug dog!"

At that moment another man entered the kitchens.

"What's all this noise, what's going on?"

"Captain, we found a stow-away," said Mr. Choo.

"A stow-away? Where is he?"

"He's under this."

The Captain half lifted the creel and took a long look at me, caught up in its netting.

"It's a dog, you idiots! Dogs are unlucky on ships. Get rid of him, throw him overboard!"

"But Captain, you can't do that!" Said Mister Wong.

"And why not?" Snarled the Captain.

"Well Captain... we can't throw him overboard... because... because... it would be wicked, very wicked."

"What?" Demanded the Captain.

"Er... well the harbour master might see us and then you in big trouble... don't want to get my wicked Captain in trouble!"

"That's very nice of you Wong, I didn't know you cared! However, we need to catch it, snatch it and dispatch it!

They don't call me Captain Nasty Nick from Newcastle for nothing. I was born nasty. Now get on with it!"

"Captain Nasty, please, please give him to me?"

"What do you want with this ugly animal? Get rid of him, or I might have to get rid of you!"

"But Captain, Sir, I can make a very fine stew with him," said the chef.

"A stew!"

"Yes Sir. It will be very yummy, very wonderful!"

"That sound rather tasty, Pug stew! Very well, we'll dine on him tonight. In the meantime, why don't you put him with those two mangey kittens you found earlier. You can cook them all together! Pug and kitten stew! Make sure it has lots of hot chilli sauce." Without another word, he left.

"Mr. Choo take him please to the pantry and lock him in."

"But Mister Wong, you're not going to cook the little fella... are you?"

"Of course not. I need time to think of inscrutable plan to keep him and those fluffy kittens safe from Captain Nasty."

"What will you do with him?" Asked Mr. Choo.

"I don't know. We see. First we keep them all safe."

Before I knew what was happening, I was disentangled from the creel and carried to the other side of the kitchen. I was then put into the pantry and the door was slammed shut. I sat on the cold stone floor of the pantry in total darkness. Well, this was it. My adventure appeared to be over. Was I about to become a Chinese take-away or part of a hot chili stew? Feeling very sorry for myself I lay my chin on the flagstone floor and covered my eyes with my two front paws.

As I lay there, I could hear the two chefs talking outside very quickly. It sounded as though they were planning something, but I couldn't understand a word. It was all Chinese to me. I listened for several minutes before I heard a sort of squeaking noise.

It came from somewhere in the pantry.

"Is anyone there?" I asked in the toughest, deepest voice I could muster.

No reply. I must be imagining things. But no, there it was again.

"Who's there?" I shouted. "Come out, show yourself, I won't hurt you!" Silence.

Nothing more was heard, and nothing moved. A light was shining from under the door which now allowed me to see a tiny bit of the pantry. Suddenly, I saw two shadows moving very slowly at the far end of the room. What was it? Feeling a little scared I backed up to the door. Then I heard the squeaking noise again.

Someone, or something, was in the room with me. Backing away from this noise, in a quivering voice, I asked again.

"Answer me, I'm not going to hurt you. In fact, I am very friendly. My Name is Mr. Barnaby, all my friends call me Barnaby."

There was now the most extraordinary outburst of high pitched screechy squeaky squeals. It sounded as if someone was laughing while at the same time playing hopscotch.

"Barnaby, Barnaby! It's us. It's us, Henry and Anna, your friends!"

CHAPTER SEVENTEEN

'THE GREATEST SHOWMAN'

Tears ran down all our little furry faces as we ran around each other filled with joy. We all talked at the same time, trying to tell each other of all the adventures that had got us this far.

They told me of the horror of being trapped in the bins that had then been put inside the smelly dumpster monster truck. How they spent the journey to the docks being thrown around amongst the rubbish in total darkness. Each bump in the road jostled them in and out of the smelly rubbish and toxic sludge. At times they could hardly breathe. When they arrived at the docks the dustbins were again lifted out of the monster truck and were then dropped into the bowel of the barge.

"You certainly had the most amazing adventure," I said. "What we've got to do now is think how we can get out of here and find our way back home. My 'Parents' leave the villa in three days and unless I'm with them I'm going to be left behind."

Anna started to cry.

"Don't cry, I'll find a way of getting us all back, I promise."

"I'm not crying for us Barnaby; I'm crying that you might lose your parents. It's all because of us."

My heart melted.

"Anna, it not your or Henry's fault. We must all keep positive.

So, let's find our way out. You two look over there, I'll see if there's a way of getting this pantry door open."

Off they went to see what they could find. The door was firmly shut, and we had no chance of getting out through it. The kittens came hurrying back but they had found nothing.

"We are stuck here." said Henry, "there is no way out!"

Just then we all heard a sort of scrabbling noise.

"What's that?" Asked Anna.

"It's coming from under the floor," said Henry.

The strange scratching noise continued. Henry was right, it was coming from under the flagstones. Just then the floor started to move as the earth between the flagstones started to part. The scratching got quicker. Bits of timber, earth, sand and cement were flying in all directions.

A hole began to appear, which then got bigger and bigger. We all ran to the far end of the pantry to avoid being hit by the flying debris and rubble. It stopped as quickly as it had begun. Everything went quiet. Nothing moved. Step by step I slowly crept towards this now massive hole. Hearing nothing, I very carefully peeked down into the hole to see what had just happened.

"Hi guys. Hope I didn't scare you?"

Enjoying his entrance and looking every bit the showman, out popped Moodywarp the Mole!

CHAPTER EIGHTEEN

'THE GREAT ESCAPE'

M oodywarp! How did you get here? I am so pleased to
see you! Henry, Anna, this is Moodywarp... he helped
me get to the port to find you. He is a very clever
mole."

"You'll make me blush," said Moodywarp.

The two kittens carefully shook his sharp little paw.

"We are very pleased to meet you," they said.

"It is my pleasure. Now Barnaby, If I'm not mistaken, we need
to get out of here pretty quickly."

"We were just wondering how to do that very thing. But we
can't find a way out of this room!"

"That's easy. We all descend into my beautifully
dug hole. The one thing that moles are good at is
tunnelling. If I say so myself, I am one of
the best. Come on, follow me. I've dug us
a passageway under the floor and into
the kitchens. Once we get there, we can
get up onto the deck, we then run down
the walkway. Now we've docked we'll be
out of here in no time and on dry land."

Led by Moodywarp, one by one we
descended into the dark scary abyss
that was Moodywarp's great escape.

CHAPTER NINETEEN

'SLEEPLESS IN KASSIOPI'

George, we can't leave!"

"Darling, I don't want to, but I've got to go back to work. Besides we can't stay here, it's booked out next week to someone else."

"I don't care. I'm not leaving here until Barnaby is found. You should be out there looking for him. He's lost and alone. He'll be starving. George, find him!"

"Darling, I know you're upset, so am I..."

"Upset... I'll say I'm upset! I've never been so upset. We must do something. I can't just sit here waiting for him to return!"

"Dorothy, everything is being done that can be done. The police are looking for him. Thanasis has asked all his friends to look out for him. He has searched all the tavernas and beaches near to here. We've put up posters with Barnaby's picture saying he's lost and that we've offered a reward. They're in all the gift shops in the surrounding villages. I think we are better staying put in case he comes home."

"George, please let's go out and have another search. I'm going mad just waiting here. We've looked around all the villages, why don't we go and search the olive groves or maybe go down to the docks?"

"Dorothy, that's over fifteen miles away and it's getting dark. It would be a long journey with his little legs, he couldn't go that far. He'll be around here somewhere, maybe he'll come back for some food."

"Well George, if you won't go, I'll go on my own! I'll just get my purse. Where are the keys to the hire car, please?"

"They are on the table by the front door. I wish you wouldn't! Oh, never mind, you win, I'll drive us to the docks. I'm not holding out much hope. I still think we should stay here and wait for him. Dorothy?"

The door had slammed, and the car had started. He heard an angry scream coming from outside. George quickly ran out the house. He knew he was in trouble. Dorothy had stormed out without him and was screaming as she drove off. Now he was even more miserable.

CHAPTER TWENTY

'WHY NOT STAY FOR BREAKFAST?'

Captain Nasty burst into the barge's kitchen with a wicked look on his ugly face. He shoved the cook, Mister Wong, out of his way and stood next to the cooking range. He lifted the lid on one of the pots.

"Are they in here?" He asked with a hideous grin.

Lifting the lid of one of the other pots he laughed.

"Or is it this one... are they in here? Well Mister Wong, there's only one pot left so I assume they must be in here... but they're not! Where are they!"

Mister Wong looked terrified and mumbled, "what is you look for my Captain?"

Looking even more villainous the Captain shouted at him, "What was it you said? You told me we would have a delicious supper. Pug and kitten chili stew. I don't see anything cooking. I'll ask you again, where are they?"

Mister Wong was visibly shaking, "I don't know, they have er... disappeared!"

"You stupid Chef! What do you mean disappeared? Mister Wight... where are they?"

Mister Wight ran behind Mister Wong, "I don't know... Mister Wong is right, they vanish!"

"Idiots! You are both idiots!"

Tiptoeing towards the pantry he whispered, "come out come

out were ever you are!"

With that, he lunged towards the pantry door pulling it open. Mister Wong and Mister Wight hugged each other... there was no one there! They really had gone!

"What we tell you, no one here. They vanish!"

Captain Nasty started throwing the eggs at the two chefs.

"I'll give you vanish!" He screamed as he threw two more eggs at them, "you idiots! They've dug themselves out. There's a filthy great hole in the floor! I'm going to tear this barge apart until I find them, and it won't be nice when I do!"

He lobbed more eggs at the chefs, hitting them both on their faces. The eggs cracked open, and the yolks slowly slid down each of their noses giving them a look of having a very unpleasant cold.

"Idiots!" He shouted again and with one final gesture he threw the remainder of the egg tray towards them, turned and left. Neither of the egg-covered chefs thought this a very funny *yoke!*

CHAPTER TWENTY-ONE

'ONE FOR THE POT'

Captain very mad, very angry. What we do now Mister Wong?"

"I don't know Mister Wight. We must find pug dog and kitties before Captain does."

They stood at the sink wiping the egg from their faces, wondering what to do next.

We were led along a dark narrow underground tunnel by Moodywarp. Eventually, we emerged from it and we crept carefully into the kitchen. All four of us hid behind a stack of boxes containing fresh vegetables.

"Mister Wight I think I have a plan. First we must find pug dog and kittens then we stuff them into our rucksacks and take them to market."

This was not sounding good. First this chef wanted to put us into a pot, then he wanted to make a chilli stew, and now he wants to sell us as meat in the market! How we were ever going to get out of this mess we didn't know.

"Mister Wong, why we stuff them and take to market?"

"It's the only way to save them from the Captain. We put them in our rucksacks and then we fib to Captain, tell him we go ashore to get fresh spices for stew. When we get to market, we set them free and Captain, he never know!"

So that was it! We weren't destined for the pot! He wasn't

going to cook us or sell us. He
was going to save us! Barnaby
had a whispered conversation
with Moodywarp and agreed
to show themselves. Slowly,
they both came out from
behind the vegetable
boxes. The two chefs
had their backs to
Barnaby. In order to get
their attention Barnaby
gave a small bark. The chefs
turned.

"Mister Wong, look, pug dog!"

"But Mister Wight, what is that
other creature?"

At that moment Henry and Anna, despite being told not to,
came out of hiding.

"Mister Wong, kittens! They come back, very cute. This other
creature is cute as well. He is a mole!"

"Mister Wight we have Zoo on ship! We need to get them
all to shore, chop chop, before Captain Nick puts them in big
pot. We need to be as quick as a Chinese spring roll. You fetch
rucksacks, I'll tell Captain we go get supplies."

At that moment, they heard the Captain's voice shouting. He
was outside the kitchen door telling his crew to pull everything
apart until the kittens and dog were found.

"Mister Wight hide them. The Captain, he outside!"

Mister Wight picked up the kittens and put them in an
enormous stewing pot. He then got hold of Barnaby and put
him in the same pot. He was just about to put the lid on it when
Moodywarp took a flying leap and landed in the pot amongst
them all. The lid covered the pot as Nasty Nick crashed through
the door and fell into the kitchen.

66

CHAPTER TWENTY-TWO

'A FUNNY THING HAPPENED ON THE WAY TO THE MARKET'

You stupid chefs! That mongrel and those furry moggies can't be found. I've had my crew search everywhere. Where are they? You must have seen them?"

"No Captain. They no here. We look everywhere."

"They have to be on this barge somewhere. It's all your fault they escaped. You two will pay dearly for this!"

Mister Wong, out of the corner of his eye, noticed the pot lid starting to lift. The head of Moodywarp peaked out.

This was not a good idea, thought Mister Wong. He quickly crossed to the pot and waited for the Captain to turn and pace the other way. Then he pushed Moodywarp's head back into the pot and firmly replaced the lid. That had been close!

"Captain sir, we need to go ashore and into market."

"I thought all our supplies were brought on board when we left Corfu?"

"Well Captain sir, we need... we need... er... some more... er... chilli. Yes Chilli!"

"Mister Wong! The chilli was for the pug stew. As you have lost the pug, never mind the kittens, we don't need the chilli. Idiot!"

"Captain, this very true... but... but we also need some... some... rum! Yes, we have run out of rum!"

"What!" Shouted the Captain. "Run out of rum! I was wrong Mister Wong... you're not an idiot... you're a great big idiot! Go and buy the rum but make sure you're back here within the next two hours. You've still got the supper to cook, whatever slop you'll serve up now."

As he said this, he went over to the giant stewing pot and looking straight at Mister Wong, lifted the lid.

"Ahhhh!" wailed the chef in a loud piercing roar as he did a backflip and landed on his bottom.

The Captain, astonished, dropped the lid back onto the pot in shock.

"What's the matter, Wong?"

Slowly getting up Mister Wong replied, "I have pain in my leg, very sudden, very painful. Sorry Captain!"

"Idiot!" Shouted back Nasty Nick and stormed off.

Quickly Mister Wong ran over to the pot and helped the gang get out. The kittens purred and Barnaby wagged his tail.

"Mister Wight, please to get the rucksacks?"

They placed one of the rucksacks on the kitchen table and carefully put the two kittens inside it. Finally, they put Barnaby, who was surprisingly heavy, into the second rucksack and placed Moodywarp carefully next to him.

"Come on, let's go, quick, quick. Don't forget, be very quiet as we go down the rickety gangway."

Quietly, they left. Trying to keep out of sight from any of the crew, they made their way from the stifling kitchens and up onto the deck. The sound of people working on the docks of Igoumenitsa could now be heard. The two chefs carried on along the deck and reached the gangway. Just as they thought they were safe the Captain appeared.

"Wong, why are you both going to the market? What are you up to?"

"I get six bottles of rum, Mister Wight, he helps."

"Idiot! Wong, you can manage on your own!"

"But Captain," cried Mister Wong, "I don't like to go to market on my own. I'm... er... scared!"

"SCARED! I give you something to be scared about!"

"Captain, sir, we also need eggs, lots more eggs as you broke many in kitchen," stammered Mister Wight.

"Very well, get off, both of you. There had better be no funny business on your way to the market. I'm watching you. Don't forget to be back here in two hours or you are going to be in big, big trouble."

The two chefs picked up their rucksacks and without looking back, ran.

CHAPTER TWENTY-THREE

'INTO THE WOODS'

Wong and Wight ran down the gangway and into the port. Deciding to get away from the barge as quickly as possible, they ran along the docks and out through the port gates.

"Now what we do?" Asked Mister Wight.

"Not very sure Mister Wong. We can't leave them here. The road is too busy, they get run over. We head out towards the market and find a nice field, we let them go, where they run free."

They followed the road around the port, passing all the big ships that were tied up and off-loading their various supplies. Further on they went. The streetlights were getting fewer and fewer, the sun had begun to set, and a beautiful moon was now lighting their way. A cloud of cicadas buzzing and clicking were drinking the sap from the tree roots and small branches. The noise was deafening. Onward they walked, eventually finding themselves crossing into a grassy wood with olive trees and a stream running along the side of it.

"This is perfect. Let us stop here," said Mister Wong.

They both took off their rucksacks and sat down next to a tormented looking olive tree. Slowly, they unzipped their sacks and Barnaby jumped out, followed by the kittens and Moodywarp.

Barnaby immediately started to run round in quick circles and chased his curly tail. Henry and Anna cuddled into each other, purring happily and Moodywarp ran round and round the old olive tree, burrowing as he did so, earth flying everywhere, ecstatic that he was once again free. Having enjoyed their newfound freedom, they gathered next to Wight and Wong, trying to show them how thankful they were. The two chefs then unpacked a selection of biscuits, fish and other goodies to leave for their new friends.

"Well Mister Wight, I think we do no more. They safe now. We must get back and cook supper for the barge's crew. Goodbye my little friends… good luck, you all keep safe."

As they walked off a tear could be seen in Barnaby's beautiful eyes. Soon, the two Chinese chefs, both a hero to the group, were out of sight.

After a long pause Moodywarp was the first to speak.

"As I see it, we have two very big problems. Firstly, we are lost, secondly, we are on the mainland and we all need to get back to Corfu Island."

"I think that is going to be easier said than done," said Barnaby. "We have to cross the sea and we don't have a boat!"

"We can't swim!" Squeaked the kittens.

Moodywarp stepped forward.

"I think we should find somewhere to sleep tonight, then tomorrow we can decide what to do. First, we should all dig into these delicious treats that our Chinese friends have left us. After we finish eating, we must find somewhere to sleep tonight."

They all set about eating the food in silence until they were all full. Barnaby was the first to move.

"Ok, we've all had a good feast, now we need to get going."

Off they all went, with Moodywarp leading, then the two kittens with Barnaby at the rear making sure the kittens didn't wander off and get lost. On they went, mile after mile. Moodywarp would stop, as his tummy was a little on the large size.

His legs were somewhat short and all this exercise was not at all to his liking. They arrived at an old Greek croft with a large adjoining barn. They quietly crept up to the barn doors and Moodywarp, being the smallest, went to look inside. There was a terrible smell of manure and the floor was covered in a very unpleasant wet sludge. Moodywarp carefully walked around the barn followed now by Barnaby.

Suddenly he realised that the kittens were no longer in front of him!

"Moody, the kittens, they've disappeared!"

"But they can't have, they were here just seconds ago!"

Fearfully, they both looked around and then they saw a slight movement on the ground. Two very wet and very smelly kittens emerged from a pool of sludge, looking sad and forlorn.

Barnaby rushed over to them.

"Are you both alright?" Asked Barnaby.

"No!" Said Henry. "Anna smells terrible!"

"You stink," cried Anna.

"That reminds me of a joke I heard... what did the left eye say to the right eye?"

"I don't know," said Barnaby.

"Between you and me, something smells!"

The two kittens rolled around on the ground laughing and getting even more dirty and smelly. It seemed they had both slipped on the smelly cow sludge that covered the barn floor and were smothered in it.

"Never mind, we'll soon get you both cleaned up. In the meantime, we should be safe sleeping in here for the night," said Barnaby.

They all found a clean dry spot to curl up on. One by one, despite the pungent smell, they all fell fast asleep. It had been a long day.

CHAPTER TWENTY-FOUR

'THE CURIOUS INCIDENT OF THE BULL IN THE BARN'

The night had a warm breeze blowing through the barn. Apart from the odd owl calling, all remained silent. The two kittens slept soundly while Barnaby and Moodywarp took turns to keep a lookout for any intruders. It was about six in the morning when the large doors were suddenly pushed open. Standing in the doorway, lit by a beautiful rising sun, were two men holding onto an enormous bull.

"Don't move a paw, in fact don't move anything," whispered Barnaby.

They lay in the shadow of a small stack of small hay bales not daring to even look at each other. The two farmers walked the bull over to a large hay rack which was fixed to the barn wall. A ring went through the bull's nose with a rope attached. They tied to the other end of this rope to the rack.

"Nikolaos, go and get the hay and while you're there bring back some mixed grain?"

"Right, I go now, I won't be long. Yannis, you be careful. The bull, he very grumpy, you keep out of way. I'll be back very quick."

Nikolaos left the barn. Yannis went over and got one of the small bales and put it in the rack. He then went back to the haystack and taking another, did the same.

"Crickey, if he takes much more from this stack we'll be seen. I think we need to move away from here," whispered Barnaby.

"I agree," said Moodywarp "...and the sooner the better! When he takes the next bale, we'll make our move. Get ready."

Nikolaos picked up one of the heavier bales between his two arms and resting it on his ample tummy once again, waddled back over to the bull. As he did this, the group led by Barnaby crept out from behind the last two bales of hay and started for the exit. Another ten yards and they were out. Just as they thought they were free, a frightening bellow emanated from a very angry bull. Staring at these four interlopers, he lowered his head and started to shake it from side to side. Hunching his shoulders, he pawed the ground with his front left foot. This was not good! This was not good!

"Run!" Shouted Moody. "Run!"

They all ran as fast as their little legs could go. The bull, seeing them, gave another fearful bellow and then charged towards them. Bolts flew out the wall, hitting the poor farmer, as the rack broke away. Out of the barn they all ran, perused by the raging bull who was now attached by a rope to a steel hay rack. On they ran, the bull, despite dragging the heavy rack, was now gaining on them. Moody, who had been leading, suddenly left the path and ran into the olive groves.

The others followed as the bull got ever closer.

"Scatter! Scatter everyone!" Shouted Moody.

The kittens ran to the left and Barnaby ran to the right. The bull followed Barnaby. On he ran. He was now very out of breath. He thought if he ever got out of this mess he really would go on a diet!

He glanced round only to see that the bull was now less than three metres from him. With one last supreme effort he leapt between two old olive trees and turned to face his chaser. He could go no further. With a blood curdling bellow the bull leapt. Barnaby closed his eyes and waited for the bull to strike. Another bellow, but this time it wasn't so much a bellow, more a... cry! Barnaby opened his eyes. A metre away was the bull lodged firmly between the two gnarled olive tree trunks. He was so big that he had got stuck between the two trees. Barnaby didn't know whether to laugh or cry! The bull bellowed again. This, Barnaby thought was his cue to run, and he did.

Having run on for a few minutes and seeing he was now safe, he sat down to work out what his next move should be. Firstly, the negatives. He was lost and had no idea where the kittens were. Moodywarp was also nowhere to be seen. Then, there was a rampant bull still after him. Now the positives... there weren't any! Instead of feeling sorry for myself, he thought, I need to find my friends. I need to get off my curly tail and go and find them. He staggered up and was immediately hit by a terrible pain in his front left paw. He gave it a few licks. His paw was very warm, and the pain was now so bad he could barely walk. For the next half an hour he limped along the olive grove shouting for the kittens and Moody. Tired and feeling sorry for himself, he stopped for a minute to give his aching paw a rest.

It was then that he saw two snakes slithering towards him. When they got close to him, they stopped. Barnaby then saw that it wasn't two snakes but one with two heads! Not only that but they were both wearing a bow tie! Both of the heads started to hiss, and their tongues flashed in and out of their wide mouths. Barnaby barked back. This, he thought, could be a lot of trouble!

"I say old boy, you're a strange looking fella!" Said the bigger snake head.

"Never seen anyone like you before," said the other head.

Barnaby, thinking if anything was strange looking it was them, so he barked again, and stared back at them.

"No need to be like that dear boy, we won't harm you!"

"Absolutely not," said the smaller one, "we were just passing, and you looked lost, so we wondered if you needed help?"

"I'm fine, thank you, Er... do you, both, live around here?"

"We live here, there, everywhere. We are free spirits. We wriggle where the mood takes us. That's right isn't it Mr. Yoda?"

"That is very correct Mr. Disney. My name is Disney, and my small friend is called Yoda. What's your name?"

"Barnaby," he spluttered in surprise.

"Well Barnaby, I'd like to ask you a question..."

"By all means, ask away," said Barnaby.

"What is a snakes favourite subject at school?"

"I don't know," said Barnaby, looking at the snake.

"Hiss-tory!"

They both wriggled about in hysterics, and then, with a glance back, slithered away.

The sun was full, and the day was getting hotter. Barnaby was not only hot, hungry and very thirsty, he was also in a lot of pain. As he limped along, he suddenly remembered the stream and quickly decided the best thing he could do was to retrace his tracks and find it.

Twenty minutes later he was sitting all alone by the gently flowing water. Placing his injured paw in the cool soothing stream he wondered if the kittens were safe and where they were now.

"Hello Mr. B!"

Turning quickly around he saw Moodywarp, Henry and Anna.

CHAPTER TWENTY-FIVE

'FOOTLOOSE'

Anna came rushing over and jumped on Barnaby's back and licked his ear.

"Barnaby, you're safe, you're safe!"

Barnaby squealed with excitement, "guys, I'm so happy to see you all!"

Moodywarp, seeing that Barnaby was limping, asked him what had happened.

"I don't know," explained Barnaby, "I was running from that bull when I suddenly got this terrible pain in my foot and now it's all numb and I can't seem to feel anything!"

"Here, let me take a look," said Moodywarp.

Barnaby carefully put Anna back on the ground, he sat down on his hind legs and put out his front left paw. It was very red and quite swollen. Moodywarp took a long look at it and then looked up to Barnaby.

"It looks pawly to me," he said with a loud chuckle.

"Oh, very funny," muttered Barnaby.

"Hold on! I think I can see the problem. This might hurt a bit so be brave."

Moodywarp took hold of the injured paw and with his sharp teeth started to nibble at it. The pain started to get worse until Barnaby could bare it no longer and let out a loud howl and fell on his side.

"Got it!" Cried Moody. "That was disgusting!" He shouted as he spat something out that was lodged between his two front teeth.

"What is it?" Asked Barnaby, who by now was heavily panting and running around in circles on three legs. Truth be told, he was being a bit of a wimp!

"It is a rather nasty thorn. They can be quite poisonous, but I think I managed to suck out all the poisonous fungus. You should be ok very soon. Put your paw back into the stream and bathe it for a few minutes."

Barnaby limped to the water's edge and put his little paw into the water. After a few minutes the feeling in his paw started to come back to life. The pain had almost gone.

"Moodywarp, you are extraordinary! A prince amongst moles! How can I ever thank you?"

"You're making me blush again! It's getting hot, let's all have a drink from the stream and then we need to make that plan for us all to get back to Corfu."

Anna started to cry again.

"Why are you crying?" Asked Barnaby.

"Because... don't you see... you've only got one more day... one more day before your 'parents' leave Corfu!"

"Yipes!" barked a suddenly very upset pug dog.

CHAPTER TWENTY-SIX

'PAL JOEY'

As the day got hotter, they carried on walking through the olive groves finding their way to the port. How they were going to find a boat to get them back to Corfu they did not know. Arriving at the outskirts of the port, the cars got more numerous, and the road started to get busier. Mopeds zoomed around, and the local villagers could be seen buying their lovely Greek bread in the local shops. They had reached the gates to the port. There was a small taverna outside. Next to it was a rubbish bin overflowing with half eaten pitta bread, kofta meatballs and kebabs.

Barnaby was the first to tuck in, heading straight for the kofta. The kittens got stuck into the kebabs.

"Aren't you having anything Moodywarp?" Asked Barnaby.

"Er... no. I'm afraid there is nothing here that a mole likes. You see we only really eat... earthworms! Sometimes, maybe for Christmas, we treat ourselves to a very small snake."

"Yuk... that's horrible... I think I'm feeling a bit sick!"

Moodywarp, not understanding why anyone would feel sick at the thought of earthworm eating, decided it was time to move on.

"Right. It's a good time to decide our next move," said Moodywarp.

"First, we need to find a boat that's heading to Corfu. Then, find a way of us all getting on board without being seen."

Barnaby interrupted, "what I suggest is when we get onto the docks, Moodywarp and I go in search of a boat and Anna and Henry stay hidden until we get back. We can't all wander around the port in daylight. We will have to wait until it gets dark. So, in the meantime let's find a place to hide."

Having found the perfect hiding place for the kittens, Barnaby went to one end of the dock, while Moodywarp went to the other. They each found a little nook to stay out of sight. They planned to meet back up with the kittens once they had found a suitable boat.

As soon as the sun had set, Barnaby came out from his hiding place and followed the road along the docks, passing signs that read 'dock A' then 'dock B' and onto 'dock C'. None of them had a sign for Corfu. On he went, arriving at 'dock D'.

Eureka! Under the sign was a list of sailing times for departures to Corfu. He looked at the timings and saw that the next ferry was at one o'clock that morning, just over three hours away.

He must go and tell the others. He started to run back to where the kittens were hiding, passing a broken wreck of a small sailboat, until he came to an abrupt stop. Standing in front of him was... him!

Now, he knew that didn't make sense, but he was staring at a pug dog and a pug dog was staring back at him. They were identical! What is going on? Who is this?

"Excuse me? Do you speak English?"

"Of course! My name is Joe. I'm here on holiday."

"I'm pleased to meet you. My name is Barnaby and I'm from England. In fact, I'm from York."

"But I'm from York as well! My 'mother', Miss Caroline, got me from a lovely woman in Oswald Twistle."

"That's where I came from. We must be related!"

"Brother!" Shouted Barnaby.

"Brother!" Barked back Joe. "So, what are you doing here?"

"It's a very long story and one that, at the moment, might not have a happy ending!"

For the next twenty minutes Barnaby told Joe all that had happened on his unexpected and extraordinary Greek adventure.

"After I escaped the bull and met back with the others, we managed to find our way here. Our problem now is to get us all on a ferry back to Corfu."

"Now it makes sense! I thought I'd seen you! Your picture is on posters all over Corfu."

"I know," said Barnaby.

"Don't you see, my 'mother' will have seen it! It won't be a problem. She is traveling over to Corfu tonight with her friend. Once she sees who you are, she'll take you onto the ferry in our car."

"That's very kind of you, but I can't leave the others. I'm afraid it is all of us or nothing!"

"Yes, I can see that might be a bit of a problem. We had better devise a plan before we go back to the car."

For the next half an hour they plotted and schemed. First Joe came up with an idea and then Moody. Both of them dismissing one thought after the other, until they came up with what they considered to be the perfect plan. Joe, who had been instrumental in forming this plan, looked pleased with himself.

"Right, Mr. B, let's get this show on the road!"

CHAPTER TWENTY-SEVEN

'ANYTHING GOES'

Moodywarp jumped up onto Barnaby's back, and hanging on for dear life, they all ran along the docks followed by Joe. Eventually, they found the place where they had left the kittens hiding. They weren't there!

"Are you sure this was the place we left them?"

Moodywarp ran up and down as if doing an Indian war dance.

"No... it's the wrong place!" He shouted. "Follow me."

He ran to the next open space and there hiding behind some oil barrels, were the two kittens. Barnaby, very relieved, introduced them to Joe.

"Very pleased to meet you," said Henry.

"Me too," said Anna.

Barnaby then went on to talk about their plan.

"I think it should work well. At the moment anything goes. Anything that will get them home."

Suddenly, Moodywarp started to make various high-pitched squeals, snorts and squeaking noises while at the same time grating his teeth. This lasted for several minutes. Barnaby was worried that the sun had got to the poor mole and he'd gone potty! The two kittens however thought it was very funny and laughed uncontrollably. "I've got it... I've got it!" Said Moody. "No! No, I haven't, that won't work! Wait... I have got it! Ok, listen up everyone, this is what we are going to do..."

CHAPTER TWENTY-EIGHT

'LAND OF HOPE AND GLORY'

Time was now moving at a fast pace.

"We had better get going, the ferry leaves in less than an hour! Everyone will be boarding soon. Anna, Henry, you both stay here and keep out of sight. I'll be back for you in ten minutes. Joe, as we planned, you lead the way."

Joe went running along the dock looking for the car park. He told Barnaby to keep close to him as he searched for the car he'd been traveling in. Passing rows of cars, caravans and motor bikes, Joe came to a sudden stop.

"This is it! This is her car."

He was standing alongside a 1978 Ranger pick-up truck. It had a beautifully painted red body with new silver wheels that were wrapped with fresh rubber.

As they stood looking at it, a loud scream was heard. "Joe… Joe! Where have you been? What have you been up to, you naughty boy! I've been so worried, you've been gone for over an hour, we've been frantic!"

A stylish woman dressed in a long, cool, hippy style flowing dress ran to him and scooped him up into her arms.

"Oh Joe, I thought I'd lost you forever. Why did you run away you naughty little pug dog?"

She was about to put him back down when she saw Barnaby

sitting quietly by the car. I don't believe it, she thought, another pug!

"Hello… and who are you?" She asked.

Barnaby came running up to her and slowly nudged his way around her ankles, chasing his tail and preening as he went.

"What a beautiful pug dog," she declared. "Joe, your friend is so handsome. Just a minute, I know who you are, you're Barnaby. You're the missing little pug from Corfu. I've seen posters with your picture on them. They're all over the island!"

At that moment an elderly, rather plump lady came striding towards them.

"Caroline, what are you doing? Oh! I see, you've found Joe, but who is this other little chap?"

"This… this is Barnaby! You remember, he's the little dog that's been missing for nearly a week on Corfu."

"Of course! He's a handsome little chap, isn't he? You found him. You clever girl. Well done Caroline! We will take him back to Corfu with us. Talking of which we need to get going or we'll miss our ferry."

Miss Caroline picked up Joe. Unlocking the car door, she put him in the front of the cab. Dame Hope Quackenbush, for that was her name, eager to help, picked up Barnaby and put him next to Joe, the two sitting on the front seat.

"I'll just go and collect our duty-free brandy." said Dame Quackenbush. "Put the windows down a touch and come and help me carry the brandy Caroline. I've been a bit naughty and bought seven bottles!"

Off they went. Once they were gone Moodywarp came out of hiding, wiggled through the gap in the window and into the cab.

"Hi guys," he said. "It's going well so far, well done Joe. Now for the second part of our plan."

"Your plan!" said Barnaby. "I don't like it. I don't like it at all. Moody, you are taking a big risk. Firstly, when the ladies see you, you might get hurt as they try to get you out the cab. Secondly, you'll be stuck in here on your own."

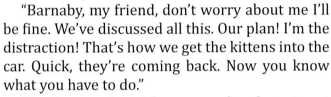

"Barnaby, my friend, don't worry about me I'll be fine. We've discussed all this. Our plan! I'm the distraction! That's how we get the kittens into the car. Quick, they're coming back. Now you know what you have to do."

The door to the pickup opened and staring at the two of them was The Dame.

"Hello Mr. Barnaby," she said in her very posh bass voice, "we'll soon get you home…" as she said this, she noticed Moodywarp. She froze. Then she gave out a long loud scream which could be heard throughout the port.

"What is the matter?" cried Caroline as she came running to the car.

"My dear it's a… it's a mouse, or worse, a rat. Get rid of it!"

As she said this, Moodywarp flipped from one side of Barnaby to the other. Then he scampered over the dashboard, ran down the gearstick and then down to the brake pedal. As if this wasn't enough Joe began to howl like a wolf in pain. The noise and mayhem combined was frightening.

Miss Caroline having kept her cool, looked on in a stunned silence. The Dame carried on shouting and screaming.

"Get it out! Get it out!"

What neither of them saw was throughout this distraction Barnaby had jumped from the car and fetched the kittens from their hiding place. The two kittens quickly climbed into the back of the pick-up and hid under an old tiger rug, complete with its big head that the Dame kept for sitting on when she went picnicking.

Moodywarp gave a last crazed lap of the driving cab and then, heading straight towards Dame Hope Quackenbush, dived out the car window and, using her head as a springboard, landed on the tarmac and took off. Falling backwards from the cab door she screamed, and her hat fell off.

She lay on the tarmac, arms akimbo, discombobulated with her dress over her head and her legs and feet waving in the air. Miss Caroline rushed over to her. Keeping calm, she helped the Dame up and rescued her hat. At the same time Barnaby took this opportunity to jump back into the pickup.

"Right," said the Dame brushing herself down. "Enough of these shenanigans we must dash to our departure gate immediately or we will miss our ferry. Caroline, you will drive."

Barnaby and Joe sitting in the front seat of the 4x4, watched as Moodywarp scampered off along the port until he could no longer be seen.

Miss Caroline put the pick-up truck into gear, and with a squeal of the tyres, sped off to the Corfu gate. She took a hard left turn, spinning the car so fast it did so nearly on two wheels. Caroline changed gear, second gear, third gear and as she was about to get into fourth gear when she saw the sign for Corfu departures. She stamped on the breaks and screeched to a holt. Dame Hope Quackenbush shot from her seat, landing in the well of the car, with Joe and Barnaby landing on top of her. The Dame, taking Barnaby's tail from out of her mouth, crawled up to her seat. Looking harshly at Caroline she declared that they had arrived.

CHAPTER TWENTY-NINE

'DAMES AT SEA'

Caroline slowly inched the truck up to the ticketing machine and punched in their pre-booked details. Name, Car registration and credit card details. All was good and the machine issued the tickets. Off they went again and this time they stopped at a glass fronted hut with two custom officers inside.

"Kalispera Madam," said the officer.

"Good evening to you too" said Caroline.

"Madam, we do checks on foreign cars crossing over to Corfu. Are you the owner of this car?"

"She is not, it is mine," snapped Hope Quackenbush.

"I see. Madam, we take look inside your car. Parakalo, I mean please you go out."

"My good man! Do I look like a criminal! I am Dame Hope Quackenbush from Yorkshire in England. I expect to be treated with respect!"

"Yes Madam. Now please, you get out from car!"

"My good man, if you think..."

"Now please Madam," interrupted the customs officer.

"Caroline, help me out the car. Let this man do whatever it is he has to."

The Dame got out with help of Caroline. The customs man went to get into the drivers seat.

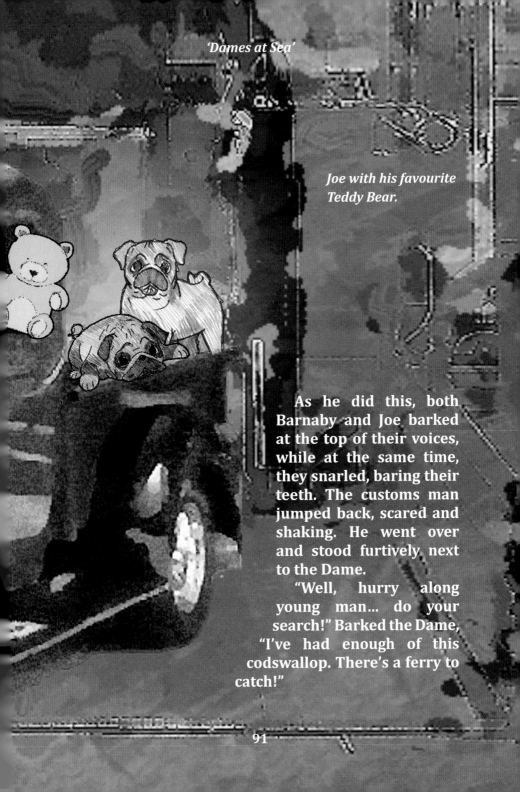

Joe with his favourite Teddy Bear.

As he did this, both Barnaby and Joe barked at the top of their voices, while at the same time, they snarled, baring their teeth. The customs man jumped back, scared and shaking. He went over and stood furtively next to the Dame.

"Well, hurry along young man... do your search!" Barked the Dame, "I've had enough of this codswallop. There's a ferry to catch!"

The customs man looked at the car, the pugs barked again, showing their teeth. He looked to the Dame.

"It's no matter. I see enough. You carry on!" With that, he went back to his customs shed.

"Caroline!" Bellowed the Dame. "We need to board our ferry! Lead on, lead on!"

They went through the entrance to 'dock D' and followed the winding track to the ferry. Once they reached the ferry Caroline drove down the rattling ramp and into the depths of the boat.

"Hope, I think our custom officer was afraid of these two very clever pugs. He soon changed his mind when he saw them!"

"Stupid man! Once we've parked let's go and find the bar, I need a large glass of red wine," said the Dame.

"I'll follow you up there in a minute. I need to give these two little chaps some food and water."

She set out a big bowl of water, then put two bowls of Royal Canin sardine and mackerel diner out for them.

Just as she was leaving to go upstairs to the lounge she turned

92

round. Then she remembered. Looking in her bag, she dug out Joe's favourite teddy bear and gave it to him.

Joe looked at Barnaby, slightly embarrassed.

"Don't worry, I've got mine but had to leave it back at the villa," said Barnaby.

Just before Caroline left, she gave them both a pat and a little treat.

"Well done you two! Look after each other and I'll see you when we arrive in Corfu."

Caroline climbed the steps up to the lounge bar and found the Dame sat at a table drinking a bottle of rather nice red wine. The sea was smooth, the moon was full. Ten minutes later the ferry set off. They were on their way back. Back to Corfu.

The Dame Hope Quackenbush and Caroline enjoying their wine.

CHAPTER THIRTY

'CHIMES AT MIDNIGHT'

G eorge! Wake up! How can you sleep?"

"Dorothy, what's wrong? It's midnight!"

"I don't care what time it is! In just twenty-four hours we have to catch our boat back to Venice and then drive home to England, without Barnaby! I can't do it! I can't go without him. We must find him!"

George went over and put his arm around her.

"Dorothy, I miss him as much as you do. We have done everything we can to find him. Nobody has seen him. I don't know what more we can do."

"George, we've got all of today for one final search. As soon as it gets light, I'm going out to have a last look. Please come with me!"

"Of course. We'll start at six, when it gets light, that's nearly six hours from now. We'll spend the whole day looking for the little fella. I've told Thanasis we'd have a last drink at his taverna to say goodbye and thank him for all his help. I said we'd be there about six o'clock tomorrow, actually that's today now! Then we can drive to the terminal and get there for ten and catch the midnight ferry. Now let us both get those few hours' sleep, or we'll never last the day."

CHAPTER THIRTY-ONE

'DIRTY ROTTEN SCOUNDRELS'

The two pugs were dozing happily in the knowledge that the kittens were now well on their way back to Corfu and their plan had worked.

Down in the parking hold of the ferry it was dark and eerily quiet. In the back of the pickup the kittens were asleep under the tiger rug dreaming of getting back to Thanasis's taverna.

From the other end of the parking area a shuffle of feet tiptoeing could be heard. Then it stopped. A minute later it could be heard again. The two kittens were woken by the strange noise and sat alert listening. Whoever it was they were on the move again, getting nearer to the pickup. The kittens wondered if Barnaby and Joe heard the noise but then realised that they were shut inside the cab and they probably wouldn't hear it. Slowly the shuffling got even nearer, then it stopped. Then they heard whispering.

"I told you we'd have fun on our holiday. This is better than breaking into cars back home in England. What do you think Dodgy, that car looks a good target?"

"Nah, we can do better than that Fingers. We need to find a nice... well, look wot we've got 'ere!"

They had just reached the Pickup.

"I think, Fingers, my man, that this is the one."

"You're right Dodgy this will be easy pickings. Let's 'ave a look in the back first. There might be something back there worth pinching."

They both walked towards the back of the pickup. The kittens, by now, were more than a little scared.

"I'm frightened," whispered Anna.

"So am I, just a little bit," said Henry.

As the two robbers started to rummage into the back of the truck, Anna came up with an idea which she whispered to Henry.

"I don't know if it will work but it's worth a try."

"I think it's brilliant," mimed Henry. "When I whisper 'now' we'll give it a go."

Slowly, the two robbers got to the end of the pickup truck. Looking all about them, checking no one was around, they quietly opened the back tailgate.

"Now!" Henry mouthed.

The two of them stood up, with Anna getting onto Henry's front shoulder. They were both under the Tiger-skin rug.

The giant head of the tiger started to rise, and the kittens wriggled to make the rug move. Slowly the 'tiger' came to life as it now stood, tossing its head from side to side.

Dodgy looked at Fingers, Fingers looked at Dodgy and then they both stared at the tiger. The tiger's large head was now thrashing even faster, while the body appeared to get taller and ferocious.

Panicking, they started to run, bashing into each other as they ran. "Run for our lives, it's a tiger! It's a tiger!"

The two kittens came out from under the tiger rug and laughed long and very loudly.

"Well," said Anna. "That was fun!"

All the commotion had woken Barnaby and Joe.

"I'd better go and check on the kittens," said Barnaby.

He climbed up on the back of the seat and wriggled his little tubby body out the opening gap in the window. Hanging on for dear life, he clawed his way to the back of the pick-up and landed on top of the rug with a thump. Seeing no one, he called out, "Henry, Anna! Where are you? are you ok?"

The tiger rug started to move; two little faces appeared.

"Barnaby! Are we pleased to see you!"

"I'm very pleased to see you! What happened?"

Talking over each other with excitement, the two recalled all that had just gone on. Henry said how clever he thought his little sister was.

"I am very impressed with the both of you," declared Barnaby. "You're both very brave. It seems our plan is working. We should be in Corfu in just over an hour. Joe is sure Caroline will drive me straight to my 'parent's' villa. Once there, you two can run back to Thanasis's taverna. In the meantime, keep very quiet and stay under this tiger rug. We don't want any of us to get caught when we are so close to getting us all home."

Barnaby climbed out of the back of the truck and, squeezing himself back through the driver's window, scrambled into the front of the pickup.

Joe pounced on Barnaby eager to hear news of Henry and Anna.

Barnaby told him of the kitten's adventure. "Not only were they brave but clever too, if a little flummoxed."

"Well, it certainly sounds as though they were very inventive," said Joe, "I guess all we can do now is sit here and wait until we dock in Corfu. Then the fun will start!"

CHAPTER THIRTY-TWO

'ON A CLEAR DAY, YOU CAN SEE FOREVER'

Will all passengers please return to their cars in the parking hold, boomed the instruction over the tannoy.

"That's us," said Barnaby as he nudged Joe awake. "We'd better get ready. They'll be on their way back to car."

Just as he said this, the heavy electric doors opened, and a queue of people entered and ran towards their cars. At the back came Caroline carrying a load of carrier bags, followed by the Dame. She was wearing an enormous floppy pink straw hat that covered her head and most of her face. She had spent an hour in the duty-free shop!

"Come along Caroline, keep up. We must get to our car."

Caroline staggered towards the pick-up carrying numerous bags containing the Dame's shopping.

She threw the bags into the back, just missing the kittens.

"Caroline can you hear your little Joe, he's snoring!"

As the two ladies got into the car the two pugs looked up and wagged their happy curly tails. The enormous car ramp at the end of the ferry slowly lowered and daylight came flooding through. Cars started to move off and soon the pickup with Dame Hope Quackenbush, Miss Caroline and two handsome pugs together with the two hidden kittens, drove off the ferry.

Once again, They were back on the beautiful island of Corfu.

CHAPTER THIRTY-THREE

'LONG DAY'S JOURNEY INTO FRIGHT'

Dorothy we must get back to the villa and do our packing. We've done our best, but no one has seen him."

"George, this is breaking my heart. I love Barnaby and I can't think of going home without him!"

George took hold of her hand. "I know, I'm just the same but we really don't have a choice. We need to be on that ferry tonight. I have to be back at work next Tuesday."

Slowly, Dorothy got back into their hire car. George had never seen her so upset and it was breaking his heart.

"I tell you what, we'll have one last look down by the dock area before we go back to the villa. It's five o'clock so that gives us another hour."

Turning on the car engine he headed down along the winding road towards the docks.

Dame Hope Quackenbush had found one of the posters that was asking if anyone had seen the lost dog, Barnaby.

"Right Caroline. It states here where this little chap lives. We need to head out from these docks towards Kassiopi. We can stop on the way and get some cold bottled water, then carry on and find Barnaby's owners. I think we need to go to the top of that winding road on our left. Yes, that's it. That will get us onto the right road."

We've not passed a single animal yet, let alone seen sight of Barnaby," cried Dorothy. "Look, there's a little patisserie, let's stop there and ask if anyone has seen him."

They both went inside the shop and speaking very bad Greek, tried to explain that they were looking for their lost dog. After several minutes of total confusion, it became apparent that, sadly, no one had seen him. They took the opportunity of buying a bottler of cold water before they left the shop.

"Right," said George, "we'd better hurry if we are going to look around the docks and get back to the villa in time."

George turned on the ignition and sped off. The road was very narrow and windy and if truth be told, George was going much too fast. As he descended the hill, a little too quickly, he saw an old red pickup coming towards him. By the time he realised there was not enough room for both cars to pass, it was too late. With his foot pressing hard on the brakes and steering his car over to the dirt and gravel on the side of the road, he just managed to stop before hitting an olive tree. Dorothy let out a little scream! George, with both hands gripping the steering wheel and with white knuckles looked up. As he did so he saw a large woman wearing an enormous pink straw hat wave at him with her fist. Then the old pickup carried on and slowly passed them by.

Miss Caroline had stopped outside the little patisserie. The Dame swallowed hard and composed herself.

"Well, some of these drivers! That man was a real Flibbertigibbet. He almost drove us off the road! Well done Caroline, if it wasn't for you, we might have ended upside down in a ditch! My nerves have gotten the better of me. Please be kind enough to fetch me a bottle of cold water from that little shop?"

Caroline was just about to pass the little patisserie.

"I'll be two minutes," she said as she got out the car and went in.

I wouldn't mind some water myself, thought Barnaby. It had been a bit too close, and the two pugs had been thrown from the front seat onto the floor of the pickup.

"That was unexpectedly exciting," said Barnaby.

"Yes, but I wouldn't want to do it again."

"Hopefully we never will. Joe, I know where we are. We're only five minutes away from the villa... five minutes from my wonderful 'parents' and it's all thanks to you Joe."

"Ah gee, I didn't do much. It was you who saved the kittens. Barnaby, I've just had a terrible thought! After our little 'off road' adventure just now I hope Henry and Anna are alright at the back? The car had to swerve quite badly, and they could have been thrown out!"

Barnaby thought long and hard. "Well, we can't do anything until we stop, then I'll climb into the back."

I am so sorry Dorothy. He's nowhere to be seen. We've been up and down these docks and there is no sign of him. I'm afraid we going to have to get back to the villa and pack."

"I understand George, but I don't think I'll ever get over losing him. This is the worst day of my life."

"We must just hope that he has found somewhere nice to stay and that he is safe."

With heavy hearts, they started back to their villa.

What's that terrible noise... and why is the car shaking like this?" Asked Dame Quackenbush.

"Oh dear," exclaimed Caroline "I think we may have a puncture. It must have happened when we were nearly driven off the road."

At that moment, a police car slowly passed them by. Caroline jumped out from the car and waved after it. At the same time The Dame pressed heavily on the car horn and flashed the lights. The police car stopped. Slowly, it backed up towards them and a young policeman got out.

"Madam, I see from your hire car that you are British. How can I be of assistance?"

The Dame started to say something when the policeman stopped her.

"Excuse, I was talking to this young lady," he said staring at Caroline. "My name is James, Sergeant James. How is it I can be of assistance?"

Caroline blushed. "Well officer, it appears we have a puncture, and we don't appear to have a spare tyre."

"For the beautiful lady, I will help," he replied. "We get you to the, how you say, car mender?"

"Very good Sergeant James. Do we go in your car?" Asked The Dame.

Sergeant James looked towards the Dame and then back at Caroline.

"I think it best Madam, if you stay here with broken car and the woofing dogs."

"OK," said The Dame, "Caroline, I'm sure we won't be long. You look after everything here."

"No Madam! I think it best if you stay here while I take this young lady with me to the car fixer. I will tell him to come and mend your tyre. Come, we go now."

With that, he ushered Caroline into his car and drove off. The Dame stood for several minutes staring after them with her mouth wide open.

CHAPTER THIRTY-FOUR

'A MIDSUMMER NIGHT'S SCREAM'

Right, I think that's everything. We're all packed. We can drop the hire car off at the ferry terminal."

Dorothy did not answer. All she could think about was Barnaby and how much she missed him.

"Darling, I hate to see you so unhappy. I'd do anything to find him but there is nothing more we can do. I've promised Thanasis that we would stop and say goodbye."

"George!" Dorothy screamed. "It's not fair!" She screamed again. "Barnaby should be with us... and all you want to do is go to a taverna!"

Then in frustration she screamed again.

"Darling, I love him as much as you do. The last thing I want is to go home without him. The only reason to go to the taverna is to thank Thanasis for all his help. We should at least say goodbye."

"You're right George, I'm sorry for screaming at you, it's not your fault. Let's get out of here and go and say goodbye to Thanasis."

George had one last check throughout the villa and satisfied they had got everything, locked the doors, put their luggage in the boot of the car and climbed in. They were off to the little beach taverna for the last time.

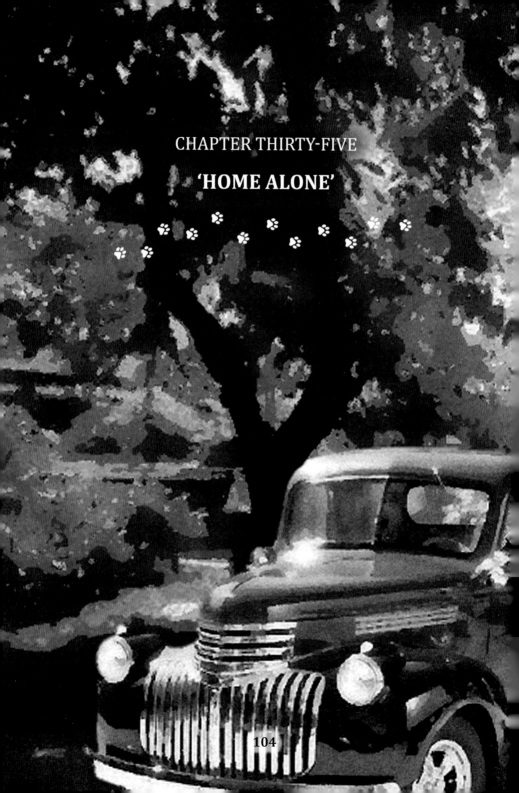

CHAPTER THIRTY-FIVE

'HOME ALONE'

It took the garage nearly two hours to fit and replace the torn tire. While they were fitting it, Caroline who had returned in the garage truck, took the pugs for a walk and then gave them some cold water. Barnaby tried to check on Henry and Anna but never got a chance. Both him and Joe were terrified that someone from the garage would discover the kittens.

Once the job was finished Dame Hope Quackenbush paid the garage and thanked them for their help. After all this kerfuffle, they were on their way again. They travelled for nearly ten minutes in silence. Then the Dame spoke.

"We are very close Caroline so slow down and let me see the name on all these villas."

Caroline slowed down and crept past each villa, stopping at each entrance gate.

"That's it!" She shouted, "Villa Kouloura... Caroline, we've found it!"

Barnaby couldn't contain his excitement. He was barking and running around the seating of the car, again chasing his tail.

"I think he's excited to be back at his home," said Caroline.

She drove the car through the gates and steered it up a very steep driveway. At the top was a narrow pass which went into a courtyard where the villa stood.

The two ladies got out of the pickup and let Barnaby and Joe run ahead. They reached the door and knocked on it loudly. No answer. They knocked again. Still no answer.

"It looks empty, and it's all locked up," said the Dame.

"It doesn't look as though anyone is staying here," said Caroline.

"I'll check at the back where the swimming pool is."

Off she went with The Dame with both pugs following. The pool was clearly not being used. All the pool chairs were folded and stacked away. There was no sign of any towels or bathing costumes.

"Caroline, I think we might be too late. It looks as though they have left!"

The Dame walked to the other side of the pool and was now looking down the cliff to the little bay with the taverna on it.

"I'm not sure what more we can do. If we can't find the owners maybe you could look after Barnaby with Joe?"

Joe, on hearing this, wagged his tail.

"You'd be very welcome," said Joe, "I'd love you to come and stay with me."

Barnaby looked up at Caroline. He had become very fond of her and now considered Joe his best friend ever. The thought, however, of never going home again, filled him with dread. All he wanted to do was to go back home with his 'parents'.

"Thanks Joe, I could not have found a better friend, but I need to find my 'parents'. I've had enough adventure for now."

Adventure! He suddenly remembered how this had all began. The kittens! They were still in the back of the pickup.

"Joe, I need your help once more... the kittens! I need to get them out of the pickup and get them on their way. If I slip away, could you keep a little diversion going until I get back?"

"Sure Barnaby, you go, I'll keep things going here. Now, a diversion? What can I do? I know!"

With that, he dived into the pool!

Caroline screamed, and then jumped in after him. After several minutes of Joe flapping about to give Barnaby time to get the kittens, he let Caroline grab him and they swam to the side of the pool.

"Please Hope, give me a hand to get out. Joe is a bit heavy!"

She raised up the pug as high as she could, while her feet flapped quickly to keep her afloat.

"Here, take him from me."

The Dame lent down to catch hold of Barnaby and just as he was in her hands, he wriggled. She tried to grab him but in doing so lost her balance and with a loud scream, splashed spectacularly, bottom first, into the pool! She looked around her, only to see her new hat drowned!

Quietly Barnaby went back towards the villa and out to the pick-up. He huffed and puffed a little but managed to climb into the back of the open pickup by jumping off the stone wall.

"Henry, Anna, are you alright?" he called. The tiger rug started to move. The heads of the two little kittens appeared.

"Barnaby! Are we pleased to see you!"

"You are both safe now. We are up on the hill overlooking Thanasis's taverna. The others are by the pool so can't see you. Jump out and head on down. I think he will be very surprised to see you both."

Barnaby, how can we ever thank you?" Said Henry.

"Will we ever see you again?" Asked Anna.

"I hope so. I know that 'The Parents' were talking about coming back here next year. The trouble at the moment is that I can't find my 'parents'!"

"What!" squeaked Anna. "What's happened?"

"I don't know," replied Barnaby. "We think that they have already gone. We've missed them!"

"That's terrible," comforted Henry. "What will you do?"

"I'm not sure yet, but I'm sure we'll come up with a plan. Now, off you go before the others get here and see you. I'll be fine. Go straight to the taverna and good luck!"

With that, he turned and went back to the pool.

CHAPTER THIRTY-SIX

'ALL'S WELL THAT ENDS WELL'

Thanasis!" Shouted George.
Thanasis ran over to George
and Dorothy and gave them both
a strong hug and kissed them on their
cheeks.

"You have news of Mr. Barnaby?
Please tell me he has been found?"

"I'm afraid not," replied George.
"We have spent all day, every day
looking for him, but it was no good.
We have to catch our ferry tonight
to get back to England. We're on our
way to the ferry terminal and have
come to say goodbye."

"That is very sad. I will keep both
my eyes open. I also ask all in our
village to keep lookout for Mr.
B. I see anything, I call you quick,
quick!"

"Thank you. You have been so kind
to us. We are both very grateful for all
your help."

"I am happy to give to you. I get you
both last drink of good Greek wine
before you go on your way."

With that, he rushed off inside the
taverna.

Barnaby padded back to the pool. Looking around he saw The Dame and Caroline standing together. His eyes bulged in amazement at what he saw. The two ladies were soaking wet. The Dame, dripping in water, held onto a now very limp pink hat and every time she moved her shoes gave out a loud squelch. Caroline was sitting on a deckchair in a pool of water, holding onto Joe.

Her long kaftan clung to her as she shivered from head to toe. Joe, on seeing Barnaby, jumped down and ran over to him.

"What happened?" Asked Barnaby in disbelief.

"It's all my fault! When you asked for a little diversion, I thought it a good idea to jump into the pool. The trouble was Miss Caroline thought I was drowning, so jumped in after me! Then she accidentally pulled the Dame into the pool as well!

I don't think she is very pleased with me!"

Dorothy and George sat at their usual table and stared out towards the beautiful sea, not speaking and not daring to look at each other for fear of bursting into tears.

They were hurting with the pain of losing their beloved pug.

Thanasis bought a bottle of Greek wine and three glasses to the table. He poured them both a glass and then poured one for himself.

"Yasou," he said, "have a safe return to your home."

"Thank you, Thanasis. Again, you have been very kind," said Dorothy.

They drank their wine and talked mostly about Barnaby. A tear fell from Dorothy's face. Thanasis stood up and clapped his hands.

"Ok, before you leave, we give one last shout, come on, stand up, all together!"

They all held hands and looking up at the stars they shouted, "Barnaby! Barnaby!"

J oe what was that?" Asked Barnaby as he ran along the wall of the pool looking down to the taverna.

"I didn't hear anything," said Joe.

"I'm sure I heard something... it sounded like someone was calling my name!"

"I'm sorry Barnaby, but I think you imagined it... I didn't hear..."

"Barnaby! Barnaby!" Came loud voices from the taverna a long way below.

"Joe... I was right! I was right! It's them, it's my 'parents'!"

With that, he did what he always did when he was happy... he ran around in circles chasing his tail. Then he leapt over the wall. They ran down towards the taverna, stopping occasionally to make sure he could hear the shouts of 'Barnaby' and then ran on barking all the way.

B arnaby! Come back! Come back!" Shouted Caroline.

"Where do you think he's going?" asked the Dame.

"I don't know... one minute he was sitting with Joe and then..."

"Barnaby! Barnaby!" They heard from the taverna below.

"What's that Caroline?"

"I think it's..."

"Barnaby!" The cry came again.

"It is! Someone is shouting for Barnaby... it must be his owners. Look! He's running down to that old taverna!"

"Then we should follow!"

"But we need to change or something. We're both soaking wet!"

"Don't be a fusspot, Caroline," snapped The Dame. "Come along, don't dawdle!" And with that, she put her pink, now wet and limp, straw hat back on and strode over to the pickup.

CHAPTER THIRTY-SEVEN

'THE LONG GOODBYE'

Sitting dejected at the rickety table, Dorothy brushed away a tear. "Thanasis, again, a big thank you."

"The wine is lovely, and we can't thank you enough but now I fear we must take our leave," said George.

They got up from their table and with a long goodbye they got into their car. Just as George was about to start the engine two little kittens jumped onto his bonnet.

"We can't let them leave," said Anna.

"I know," said Henry. "I'm sure Barnaby must have heard them calling him. He'll get here soon. In the meantime, we need to keep them here until he does!"

Thanasis, seeing the kittens, ran over to the car.

"The kitties, they come back," he sang with joy. "You are both safe and well." He explained to George, "these are the two kittens that lived by my dumpsters. I thought they were gone, never to be back!"

George shook his hand.

"I'm very pleased for you, that's great news. Thanasis, I'm really sorry but we must leave, or we'll miss the ferry. Could you take them off my bonnet?"

"Of course. Come on kitties, come and have good Greek food."

Tempting though this offer was, Henry and Anna didn't move.

"Thanasis, we must go!"

"Of course. Come on, you leave nice people's car."

They both looked at him and then climbed up onto the roof of the car.

"Come down here! Please, both get off car roof!"

Henry and Anna pretended not to hear and looked the other way.

"Please, you start your engine, that make them come down."

George started the engine but still they did not move. He pressed the car horn. Still, they didn't get down.

"Dorothy, I'll drive very slowly and see if that makes them move."

The hire car started to move forward.

"Hang on!" Meowed Anna, "we must keep them here until Barnaby arrives."

The car moved forward again and this time the two kittens lost their balance. Henry was the first to jump from the roof followed by Anna who landed on top of him.

"Oh dear," said Henry, "Barnaby will be too late."

"Ok, we're off," said George and started to move forward.

"No!" shouted Dorothy. They had climbed under the car. George revved the engine and when that didn't work he got out of the car.

"Dorothy... look! Do you see what I see?"

Dorothy gave out a loud gasp! There, sat in the headlights, with his tail wagging, was Barnaby!

For several seconds everybody stood motionless, just staring at each other. Dorothy rushed out of the car, and as she did so Barnaby took a flying leap towards her, landing in her arms. George, with tears streaming, patted and stroked him.

Thanasis started to do a Greek dance, the two kittens ran out from under the car and purred and squealed with joy. Then the old pickup came rushing down the road and stopped outside the little taverna. Stepping out was the Dame, looking more than a little strange in her wet clothes.

By now Dorothy was overcome with joy as she kissed and cuddled Barnaby. George was still in a bit of a daze.

"Excuse me, but can one assume that this little chap is yours," bellowed the Dame over the cacophony of voices.

"Yes... yes he is! His name is..."

"Barnaby!" The Dame replied.

"That's right," grinned Dorothy, "but how do you know?"

Caroline, who had now got out of the pick-up answered. "This is my little pug, Joe, and he was the one who found Barnaby. They have been on the mainland in Greece."

The Dame continued, "I remembered the posters I had seen of him when we stayed here last week. As we were coming back to Corfu, we thought it a good idea to bring him with us. We bundled him into our old jalopy and arrived earlier today. Joe has been looking after him and, well, here we are!"

"How can we ever thank you! I thought we would never see him again!" Dorothy said, almost crying.

"Think nothing of it... he's quite a character, very like Joe."

"Drinks! We have drinks! We celebrate!" Sang Thanasis.

Holding firmly onto Barnaby, George explained that they had to get going or they were sure to miss their ferry. They quickly exchanged emails promising to keep in touch. Dorothy would send updates from Barnaby and hoped that Joe would do the same and write to Barnaby.

Barnaby made a sudden break, running to the dumpsters.

Dorothy screamed, "George, get him, he's running away!"

George ran towards Barnaby and then stopped.

"Look! He's not running away... he is saying goodbye!"

Sat on the dumpsters were Henry and Anna.

They couldn't... could they? Surely not! But... they were saying goodbye! It was almost as if they were planning to meet up again next summer!

And indeed, that was exactly what they were doing!

114

CHAPTER THIRTY-EIGHT

'LA LA LAND'

Barnaby and 'The Parents' arrived at the port with minutes to spare.

Quickly boarding, they went straight to their cabin. Dorothy opened a tin of juicy chicken chunks for Barnaby and then fetched him some cold water.

"Dorothy," said George hesitatingly, "do you fancy a quick nightcap before we turn in for the night?"

"That would be a lovely idea, just what I fancy... but what about Barnaby?"

They looked over to him and saw that he had jumped up on the bunk bed and was now fast asleep snoring his little head off.

"He'll be fine... he won't even know we've gone. We won't be very long."

Quietly, the two of them left the cabin, while Barnaby, in the land of nod, continued to snore.

Ten minutes later, Barnaby woke up. He was alone!

Where had they gone? He was starting to panic when he heard a voice.

"Don't worry Mr. B, they've gone for a drink, they'll be back soon."

Barnaby looked up at the top bunk. There sitting on the edge of the bunk bed sat... Moodywarp the Mole!

"Moodywarp! What are you doing here? How did you get here?"

"It's a long story," said Moodywarp.

"You'd better hurry up and tell me! 'The Parents' will be back soon."

"When I say it's a long story, that's just what I mean! But no matter, we have plenty of time."

Barnaby nearly choked.

"Plenty of time! Moodywarp, you're in La La Land... when 'The Parents' get back they'll see you! It could be any time now!"

"Let me speak! I really enjoyed being with you on our little adventure."

"I loved every minute of it. It was very exciting but now you must go, you'll get caught," shouted Barnaby.

"As I was saying, before you interrupted me, I've enjoyed myself so much I've decided, as you can now see, to travel back to England with you!"

"Moodywarp! What? that's wonderful, but supposing you get caught!"

"Barnaby, you should know me by now, I don't get caught! So," he whispered, "this is the plan.... my plan!"

As he said that, they both heard the key turning in the cabin door... 'The Parents' were back!

THE END... or is it?

116

Watch out for BARNABY'S next adventure

BARNABY
AND THE
BUMPTIOUS BURGLARS

Barnaby and his friend Joe overhear two villainous burglars plotting to rob the village post office.

As he races against time to stop them he crosses paths with a Unicorn who has had his horn stolen.

A giant crow called Pete the Pickpocket and a bath in a giant bowl of spaghetti!

~ • ~

ON SALE APRIL 2022